12: TASH AND THE FORTUNE-TELLER

"Show me your palms. Both of them," Gypsy Tirrasana instructed in the same breathy voice.

I obediently did as I was told, without saying anything, because I wanted to believe that this could be for real. It filled me with a sense of magic and wonder. Her eyes were on mine and I suddenly had the feeling that she knew what I was thinking. It was like being trapped, yet there was no turning back, so I sat there, heart pounding, wondering what I was about to hear.

Also in the Café Club series by Ann Bryant

The CAFÉ Club

12: TASH AND THE FORTUNE-TELLER

Ann Bryant

Hippo

Scholastic Children's Books,
Commonwealth House, 1–19 New Oxford Street,
London WC1A 1NU, UK
a division of Scholastic Ltd
London ~ New York ~ Toronto ~ Sydney ~ Auckland

First published by Scholastic Ltd, 1997

Copyright © Ann Bryant, 1997

ISBN 0 590 19564 6

Typeset by TW Typesetting, Midsomer Norton, Somerset

Printed by Cox & Wyman Ltd, Reading, Berks.

Chapter 1

Hi! I'm Tash. I'm the one they call the peacemaker. It's certainly true – I hate it when people are arguing around me, or even if they're just not getting on very well. I've got five good friends, who are thirteen and live in Cableden like me. Just as they call me the peacemaker, they've got tags too.

I'll start with Fen, short for Fenella Brooks, my best friend. We call her the ambitious one. Fen was responsible for getting us all jobs in her aunt Jan's café in Cableden High Street. We all take turns to work for two hours after school, and the sixth person works for four hours on a Saturday. We have a rota, so we all get to have a turn at doing a Saturday, which is fair, because you earn more money on a Saturday.

Back to Fen, though. She's quite tall and thin, with shoulder-length brown hair and freckles.

She's also got lovely bone structure. She's very strong willed and single-minded and she's very fond of me, goodness knows why. I haven't got half the drive that Fen's got. I don't look anything like Fen, by the way. I'm altogether much darker and my hair is a bit shorter and layered. Out of the six of us I've got the second shortest hair.

The one with the shortest hair is Andy, the daring one. Andy's real name is Agnès, which is a French name that you pronounce *Ann-yes*. Andy is half French, you see. Her mother is French and her father is English. Andy's hair is cropped and very dark. Her skin is dark, too. Her colouring is the most like mine out of the six of us, but our characters are not at all similar. Even though she's small, she's really tough, and there's nothing she wouldn't dare to do.

Andy's best friend is called Leah Bryan. Leah is the musician. She plays the violin and the piano and she's really, really talented, but she doesn't believe anyone who tells her that. Leah is very pretty with long, fine pale hair down to her waist. Her face is quite pale too and even her eyes are a sort of palish blue. Leah worries about everything. She's even worse than me for worrying, and that's saying something!

Lucy Edmunson – Luce for short – is the crazy one. She's very bubbly and full of fun and always getting into trouble. Her hair is dark blonde with a touch of auburn, and very curly indeed. Luce has also got freckles. Her best friend, Jaimini Riva, has quite a job trying to keep Luce under control!

Jaimini is the complete opposite of Luce. Her hair is black and straight and almost as long as Leah's. She's got very dark skin because her father is black and her mother is white. Although Jaimini is very beautiful, we call her the brainy one, because the lucky thing has got brains *and* beauty! Luce is always moaning about how unfair it is and how God must have got mixed up when he was handing out good things, because he gave Jaimini too many. You pronounce Jaimini, *Jay-m-nee*, by the way.

So that's the six of us who make up the Café Club. We all go to Cableden Comprehensive and we're usually very relieved when the school day is over and we're free to go down to the café to have a Coke or something, and a chat. We often all go down there, even if it's not our turn to work. There's a lovely atmosphere in the café, you see. Sometimes one of us has a club or sports practice or a violin lesson or something which prevents us from going, though. In my case it's usually because I've got to look after my little sister, Peta.

Peta is just three and she can be a real handful. All my friends think she's really sweet and very entertaining, but when you've got to live with her, believe me, it's not quite as entertaining as they think! I've also got an older brother, Danny, who's fifteen and doesn't look anything like me. He takes after Dad with his grey eyes and blond hair. I take after Mum, and Peta is like a cross between the two of our parents.

What I haven't told you yet is that Mum and Dad are divorced and we don't see Dad any more. Peta wouldn't know him from Adam because she was only a baby when Dad left. I can remember him very clearly, though. Sometimes I feel sad about not having a dad around, but most of the time I'm just grateful for what I've got because we're a happy family, and Mum's a brilliant mother. When Dad lived with us, he and Mum were always arguing and it used to really upset me. It's much more peaceful now. Maybe that's why I like everything to be peaceful all the time, because I hate remembering the time of those awful rows.

Anyway, back to today. It was not one of those days when I had to babysit Peta after school, and the six of us were all walking down to the café. It was Jaimini on duty so she went in through the back door to the kitchen and the rest of us went in through the main door to the café.

The first person we saw was Jan. Jan is forty-one, slim and fit. She moves around at that café at a hundred miles per hour and runs the place really well.

"Hi, girls."

She smiled and glanced at us all, weighing up in an instant who was missing.

"So it's Jaimini on duty, is it?" she said. "I hope she's feeling strong. There seem to have been so many customers in today."

It was true that the café was fairly crowded and when we'd all sat down at a table for six we decided to play the game of looking round and guessing amongst ourselves what the various customers were called and what job they did and things like that. Fen, in particular, usually invents amazing life histories for people.

"Drinks, girls?" came Mark's cheery voice as he approached our table, pen poised, ready to take our order.

Mark is one of the part-timers who's on at the same time as us. He's seventeen and is working at the café to earn extra money while he's training to be a Martial Arts instructor. He's already a judo expert and takes evening classes. We all like Mark, he's so gentle and kind, even though he's very big and tough-looking.

"Two Cokes and three lemonades," piped up Luce.

"How do you know what we all want?" Fen asked her indignantly.

"I don't. I was just guessing to save time," Luce answered with a big grin for Mark.

5

"Well, I want Coke," Fen said, also looking at Mark.

"And I want lemonade, please," Leah said.

"Make that two," said Andy.

"No, three," I put in.

"And mine's a Coke, so that's exactly what I said, isn't it?" Luce pointed out, sitting back triumphantly and folding her arms.

"Lucky guess," Fen insisted.

"Whatever," Luce answered, losing interest in typical Luce fashion, because she'd obviously spotted a boy she fancied.

"Look!" she breathed, clutching my arm as I happened to be sitting next to her.

"Your nails are digging in," I pointed out.

"But you're not looking," she went on, straining to see over Fen's head, while clutching my arm even tighter.

"You're going to draw blood if you carry on like this, Luce," I told her amazingly calmly, considering the agony I was in. I don't know why I bothered because she hadn't even heard me. All her senses were tuned into the tall, dark guy, who was at least in his early twenties and was sitting across the café at a table on his own.

Fen decided to intervene. Without saying a word she got up, walked round to Luce and clutched her arm in exactly the same way that Luce was clutching mine.

"Ouch! What are you trying to do? Claw me to death?" Luce exclaimed, her eyebrows knitting together in a fierce black line as they always do when she's puzzled or cross.

"That's what you're doing to Tash, Luce," Fen answered.

"Oh, sorry, Tash! Why didn't you say?"

We all groaned at that but nobody bothered to answer.

"Bet he's an athlete," Luce went on happily, oblivious to everything around her except the tall, dark stranger. "Probably a famous one," she added.

"He sings in the church choir," Leah informed her calmly. "I've seen him there, and once I got talking to him and he told me he was sending off twenty-five job applications per week, so for all we know he may still be unemployed."

"Church choir?" said Luce, rather faintly. "Maybe he's not quite as attractive as I thought," she added, her eyes swivelling round to see if there was any other talent around.

"What about those two women over there?" I asked, to change the subject, because I could just feel that Fen was about to accuse Luce of being "churchist" or whatever the word is.

"I guess she cooks for the Princess of Wales," said Fen.

"The Prince of Wales more like," Andy said.

7

"Well, one or the other," said Fen. "Royalty anyway."

"No, I meant the Prince of Wales pub," Andy the cynic explained, which made us all burst out laughing.

"Yeah, both those women are employed by the Princess of Wales, but they have to be very discreet about it, otherwise they'd be hounded by the press all the time," Leah said, getting into the story.

"And that good-looking bloke is a private detective," Luce added, returning to the object of her attraction. "You see how he's pretending to read that newspaper? Well, he's not really, because he's employed by a very rich man to follow that man's wife and find out where she goes every Monday afternoon."

"Yeah, and there she is," Andy continued, giving the faintest of nods at a woman also sitting on her own at the next table to the man.

As soon as we saw who Andy was looking at, we had to stifle our giggles because this woman was about fifty-five with a great big headscarf on and tons of make-up. She was quite fat, and wearing a very gaudy trouser suit in pink and purple velour.

"He's smiling at his newspaper," Luce hissed. "Anyone'd think he heard what you said just then, Andy," she went on excitedly. "Maybe he's got extrasensory perception or something, because there's no way he could have heard what you said, and yet he's definitely got the joke. Look."

We all dutifully looked, even though we thought Luce was probably grossly exaggerating as usual. Funnily enough, though, it *did* look as if he'd got the joke, because he gave us a quick grin, shook his head slowly, as though we were all mad, then returned to his newspaper.

"Stop staring, Luce, for goodness' sake!" Fen said.

"Yes, stop staring," said Jaimini, appearing suddenly at our table. "I can't take you anywhere, Luce. What's she staring at now?" she added, to Fen.

"Give you three guesses," replied Fen dryly.

"OK. I've got it in one," Jaimini said, as she glanced quickly round the café, and her eyes alighted on our private detective.

"How's it going, Jaimini?" I asked, to change the subject again.

"Mountains of washing-up," she replied. "I'd better get on with it. I just came out for a break, and to see what you lot were up to."

"We're up to our eyes in mysterious customers," Luce replied, smiling at Jaimini.

"See you later then," said Jaimini, going back to the kitchen. "Behave yourself, won't you, Luce?" she added.

"Don't I always?" Luce answered with another smile.

After that, the game fizzled out and we began to talk about the fair that had arrived in Cableden for three nights.

"Who's going tonight?" Fen asked.

"Me," I answered.

"OK, I'll come with you," Fen said.

"Let's all go," Andy proposed, and Leah and Luce agreed immediately.

"What about Jaimini?" asked Leah.

"I'm pretty sure Jaimes can come," Luce told us.

So a few minutes later we all went off our separate ways to get our homework done, which would then leave us enough time to go to the fair. The meeting time was fixed for seven-fifteen.

"By the big wheel," said Luce.

"What if there isn't a big wheel?" asked Fen sensibly.

"By the thing that looks most like a big wheel, then," said Luce.

Again we all rolled our eyes, but decided to stick with that, as nobody could think of anything better.

When I got home, it was to find the place in chaos because Peta had a friend for tea. It was a little boy called Tom, and the two of them had wound each other right up.

"Whatever's happened here, Mum?" I asked, going through from the kitchen to the sitting room and finding not a soul in sight, but the room looking as though a bomb had hit it.

Mum came clattering downstairs with Peta on one hip and Tom on the other.

"I fink Mummy's made a big mess in here," Peta told me gravely.

"Can you help me clear it up, love?" Mum said, giving me an apologetic look and ignoring Peta's little observation. "Tom's dad'll be here in a minute. He'll think we live in total squalor if he comes in to this."

So for the next five minutes Mum and I whizzed round, putting the room in order. We tried to get Tom and Peta to help, but their idea of clearing up wasn't quite what Mum had in mind, so in the end she sat them down in front of a video.

"Where's Danny, Mum?"

"I'm not sure. Maybe he's got a match or something. I thought he'd be home by now."

Mum has always been pretty casual with Danny and me. She seems to give us more rope than most parents do, but in return she expects us to be totally honest, and not to abuse her trust. I've already decided that when I've got children of my own, that's how I'm going to bring them up too.

I was on the point of going up to my room to do my homework when Tom's dad turned up. He was about the same age as Mum and looked really nice. I know it's a terrible thing to admit, but every time I see a man of about Mum's age I start working out whether or not he'd make a suitable partner for her. Danny and I once had a horrible jolt, though, when we thought Mum was going to marry someone called Jim who had the most obnoxious children under the sun. Thank goodness Mum changed her mind, but every time I'm considering whether someone is suitable for Mum, I always look at the children first.

Tom seemed to be quite sweet. It was Peta who wound him up.

"This is my daughter, Tash," Mum was saying. Then she turned to me. "And this is Ian, Tom's dad."

We smiled and said hello, and it suddenly occurred to me that Ian was probably perfectly happily married. Just because it was the father coming to pick up the child from his friend's house, didn't mean to say that he was a single parent. Shame, because he was scoring quite highly on the Dad-ometer.

"Would you like a cup of tea, or … anything?" Mum asked.

"I'd better be going actually," replied Ian. "I've got more work to do after this one's in bed."

"OK. Another time then," said Mum, and I thought how pretty she looked, standing there in her jeans with nothing on her feet and no make-up on. Even her hair was a mess, but she still looked lovely. I glanced at Ian to see if he thought so too, but it was impossible to tell. Because I've always been pretty obsessed with the fact that Mum is a single parent, I've studied men quite a lot. With some men it's really easy to know what they're thinking, but others keep their thoughts and feelings totally hidden. Ian fell into this second category.

"What does Ian do?" I asked Mum, as casually as I could, after he'd gone.

"He's in business," Mum replied, rather vaguely I thought.

I was dying to ask if Ian was a single father, but I didn't want Mum to know how my mind was working, so I resisted the temptation and did my homework instead.

At seven o'clock I set off for the fair. Mum said I had to be back at nine-thirty at the very latest. Danny still wasn't home from school when I left, and I could tell Mum was just beginning to get worried. Danny's fifteen and very independent, but all the same, it wasn't like him not to have at least phoned Mum.

As I went through the entrance to the fair, the first person I saw was Leah with her sister, Kim.

Kim is fifteen, and she's really good-looking, with long straight hair and an excellent figure. All the boys fancy her, but it's my brother Danny she's going out with. I don't think Danny can believe his luck.

"Hi, Tash. Is Danny coming?" Kim more or less pounced on me.

"Danny hasn't appeared at home at all today," I told her, which made a big frown cover her face. "Have you seen him?" I went on.

"I saw him after school. He walked me home, then he said he was going straight home himself because he'd got tons of work to do. We arranged to meet here at seven o'clock."

"Oh well, you know Danny," I said, feeling suddenly very uneasy, but at the same time not wanting to make Kim worry. "Maybe he met one of his friends and they're working together at the friend's house or something."

"He would have phoned your mum, wouldn't he?" Kim pointed out perfectly correctly.

"Don't worry, I'm sure he'll be along soon," I quickly said, still feeling anxious.

"Tash ... you're not ... covering for him, are you?" she asked me.

I didn't get what she meant at first. "Covering? Why would I do that?"

"He's not got someone else, has he?"

"Oh, no! Definitely not," I assured her. "He'll

be along soon, you'll see."

After that we spotted Luce standing by a tent with GYPSY TIRRASANA written in huge, glittering letters over the entrance.

"I thought we were supposed to be meeting by the big wheel," said Fen, rushing up to join us with Andy. "What are you standing by a tent for?"

Luce looked at Fen as though she pitied her for her severely subnormal brain powers, and pointed at the tent without saying a word. On her face was an expression of long-suffering patience.

"What?" asked Fen, as the rest of us cast our eyes over the tent, also puzzled.

"There," said Luce. "A wheel, OK?"

We all drew closer to the tent and, sure enough, just under the T of Tirrasana, was a little wheel of fortune.

"Oh, sorry, I didn't realize it was a competition to see who could find the very smallest, least obvious wheel in the fairground," Fen retorted sarcastically.

"Well, there aren't any other wheels, are there?" Luce came back indignantly.

"Only that one over there," said Fen, indicating a half-size big wheel, which nevertheless was still huge and had a big sign over it saying WHEELAWAY.

"Well, I didn't see that," Luce mumbled.

"Where's Jaimini anyway?" I asked, quickly changing the subject.

"She can't come. Her parents didn't want her working until six and then going out again so soon after, so she's probably coming tomorrow. I'm going to see if I can come again too."

"Who fancies a go on that wheel thing?" asked Andy.

"No fear," Leah and I replied at exactly the same moment.

"I will," said Fen, so off they went.

"I'm going to buy some candyfloss, then I'm going to try and win a goldfish," Luce informed us as she marched off into the crowd. "See you back here in ten minutes."

Leah and I both stared at the gypsy tent for ages. I was wondering whether to go and have my fortune told.

"Mum always says it's rubbish, but I wouldn't mind having my fortune read anyway," I said eventually.

"I'll come with you," Leah agreed instantly. But when we got inside, a very dark, swarthy man told us that Gypsy Tirrasana would only see one person at a time, so Leah stayed outside. I felt quite nervous standing there, waiting to be told to go into the inner tent. I didn't know if I had to wait because there was someone else in there having their fortune told, or whether it was just because Gypsy Tirrasana wasn't ready.

After a few moments a little bell rang. I would have giggled if I hadn't felt so nervous, because it reminded me of a doctor's waiting room. As I entered the inner room, though, any faint ripples of mirth I might have felt immediately dissolved, because it was like entering another world. At first I could only see wreaths of pink coloured smoke, which seemed to be moving round and round very slowly and made me feel almost dizzy. Then, as my eyes got used to the atmosphere, I could make out sudden flashes of glittering, glistening silver and gold, then tiny sparklets of bright red and emerald green. I suddenly realized I was surrounded by shimmer balls of all shapes and sizes, which were suspended from the flat top of the tent. The only light in the tent was from candles, but there was a wonderful smell of burning incense.

"Come and sit down," a soft breathy voice came out of the smoke.

I walked slowly forwards, and as I did so I suddenly understood what people meant when they said that something took their breath away. The sight of the woman at the table with her crystal ball did exactly that to me.

She was wearing a long, black and gold dress and a cloak of the same colour. The clothes were so huge, and full of folds and folds of material, that I couldn't tell what shape she was at all. Red and gold chunky jewellery hung over the folds, and enormous loopy earrings fell right to her shoulders. Her hair was the shiniest, blackest hair I'd ever seen and it framed her face in a big cloud of billowing ringlets that would have made even Luce's hair look thin and fine. Her face was covered, except her eyes, by something like a yashmak that Arab women have to wear. Her eyes were very piercing. That's all I can say about them. I couldn't tell what colour they were or anything because the light was too dim, and the smoke made it even more difficult to see.

What I couldn't understand was why I wasn't coughing, but it can't have been proper smoke otherwise I would have been practically choking by then. It was so mystical and magical in that tent, I absolutely loved it. I couldn't stop staring at the gypsy's eyes. They mesmerized me and wouldn't let me look away.

"Show me your palms. Both of them," she instructed in the same breathy voice.

I obediently did as I was told, without saying anything, because I wanted to believe that this could be for real. It filled me with a sense of magic and wonder. I wasn't like Mum. I didn't want to dismiss the whole fortune-telling business as a load of rubbish. If I gave away no clues at all, and something she said about me was true, or came true, then I'd really *know* there was some truth in it, wouldn't I? I'd paid three pounds fifty, so I couldn't afford to think it was rubbish, anyway. Her eyes were on mine as these thoughts were passing through my mind, and I suddenly had the feeling that she knew what I was thinking. It was like being trapped, yet there was no turning back, so I sat there, heart pounding, wondering what I was about to hear.

Chapter 2

She only held my hands, she never touched them by running her fingers along the lines or anything like that. She just stared at my palms and every so often her eyes came up and met mine, then she stared hard at me for several seconds before looking back at my palms again. After that her eyes rested on the crystal ball on the table in front of her. I studied the crystal ball too, even though it was rather blinding, then I realized that all over her table were tiny drawings of faces which all wore different expressions. Some looked happy, some sad, some in pain, some angry. Because I'd been staring at the crystal ball, little spots of bright light blotted out some of the faces which made them look grotesque. I began to feel myself sweating.

"There is a stranger coming into your life ... a man," the gypsy suddenly began in a very low voice, so soft I had to strain to hear her. "I see water ... something about water ... and trouble ... for you. This man *is* trouble. Trouble and water ... deep water ... such a sad end."

I wanted to ask her to tell me more about the man. How old was he? What did he look like? But on the other hand I didn't want her to hear my voice, because I didn't want her to know anything about me that might give her any clues.

"You worry, my dear..." Her eyes looked accusingly at my palms as though it said "I WORRY" across them in large, bold letters. Then a second later, she was looking at my face again. "Don't you? Hmm?"

I nodded.

"You don't like unrest ...you prefer peace ... don't you ... hmm?"

I gulped and nodded again.

"But don't make waves, hmm? Don't go looking. Don't do anything." Beginning to wonder whether I could get away with doing nothing but nodding, I nodded once again, then waited as her eyes went back to the crystal. "And who is this little child, I wonder? Is it a boy or a girl? I'm not sure. But the child is in danger. Someone is helping to save the little child... More than one person is trying to help ... poor little child."

This time her eyes seemed to be trying to gouge out a hole in the crystal ball, she was studying it so hard.

"Hmm ... long lines of traffic ... in the way ... long. Aha! You *are* in demand. I see you trying to rescue a little animal now. You are trying, but you can't do it on your own..."

I wanted to scream at her to stop. This wasn't what I'd been expecting. I was hoping to be told I'd have a long and happy life, three beautiful, bright children, a wonderful husband and a fantastic career.

"And here we have a lady ... and she is happy. She is happy with you ... because you are learning something very, very well. You are so interested and so captivated by this..."

This what? I was dying to ask, but I managed to restrain myself.

"Yes, she is pleased with you ... and she wants to help you ... and she knows you will succeed in the future. And so do I. See this line..."

I studied my own palm closely, but found myself concentrating on her nails instead. They were perfectly clean and neatly cut. It surprised me that they weren't varnished in a gaudy shade of red or a glittery exotic green or something. I couldn't see her fingers at all because she wore black, very fine, almost see-through fingerless gloves.

"This line is long and strong and deep ... and it is your success. Congratulations, my dear."

I managed to smile at her then, mainly with

relief because at long last she'd told me something good. I couldn't actually tell if she was smiling back or not, which was odd because you can usually tell from a person's eyes whether or not they're smiling, even if you can't see the rest of their face at all. But in this case, her eyes were impossible to read.

"Good luck," she said, as she sat a little further back in her chair. I took that as a signal that my reading was over, so I thanked her and stood up. Turning to leave the tent I felt as though I was sleepwalking. I couldn't see the flap of the tent that I had to go through to get into the outer tent bit, so I made my way slowly towards where I thought it must be, and gradually it took shape in the gloom. I was about to go through it, when she coughed.

Turning back to face her, I was blinded by the flashes of light from the shimmer balls. Out of the haze of pink smoke came her voice, "I see a boy now. A nice tall boy. A blond boy. He's older than you. He has a lot of time for you."

Although I couldn't see her face at all, I felt certain from her voice that she was smiling, but I couldn't decide if she was genuinely happy for me that it looked as though a boyfriend was about to enter my life, or whether she was somehow mocking me with her words. I wished she hadn't said that last bit. It spoiled the rest of the reading.

I just wanted to get out then, so I shot through the flap and the swarthy man nodded at me as I plunged into the outside world, feeling the exact same feeling I'd once felt when I'd gone on a very scary ghost train, then emerged into the glaring light of day to find the world carrying on as normal. Only now, of course, it was beginning to get dark.

"Tash, you look awful! What did she say?"

That was Luce. The others were all there too, bombarding me with questions.

"What was it like?"

"Did you believe her?"

"Got any tall, dark strangers about to appear?"

"A man..." I managed to utter, but I felt so shell-shocked that I didn't have the energy to say anything more.

"Are you OK, Tash?" That was Fen. She had moved to my side and was looking really concerned. You see, Fen and I share a very big secret. None of the others know this about me, but I'm an epileptic. That means that occasionally I have fits. The fits I get are actually called absences because my epilepsy isn't very bad. What happens is that I sort of tune out completely for about twenty seconds and when I wake up, as I call it, I don't have the faintest clue what's been happening during the time I was absent. It's no different from suddenly falling asleep, except my eyes don't close, they just go peculiar and distant.

Fen would never ever let the others know about my epilepsy, and it was a great comfort to me to be sure that I'd always got Fen to look after me just in case I ever *did* have a fit in public. I once went through a period of having quite a few absences because my medication wasn't sorted out properly. But now I've got the right medication, I hardly ever have any.

"I'm fine," I assured her, with a grateful smile so she wouldn't worry about me any more, but glancing round at the others I realized I must have looked far from fine, because they all looked so concerned. I thought I'd better pull myself together and try to act a bit more normally.

"It's so smoky and weird in there," I began to explain. "And Gypsy Tirrasana is totally over the top. She's wearing one of those yashmak things so you can only see her eyes. And she really stares hard into her crystal ball."

As I was saying this I was actually thinking something completely different, but I couldn't quite admit it. You see, in a way, I didn't really think she was over the top at all. Her dress certainly was, but she herself was not. She'd scared me. That was the simple truth of the matter.

"But what did she predict for you?" asked Leah.

"Well, first she talked about this strange man, who was going to have something to do with water and would cause trouble and get me in deep water, or something."

Luce's eyes widened and she gasped. I instantly regretted having launched in like that. I felt as though as I was telling someone else's secrets. Andy's words then made me feel that even more.

"I bet if you questioned every man at this fair, you'd find at least half of them have got something to do with water."

"Don't be such a cynic," Leah rounded on her, which was quite strong for Leah. "Go on, Tash. What else did she say?"

I decided just to give them the bare bones.

"She said that a little child, which could be a boy or could be a girl, was in danger, and people would be trying to help save it."

"Covering all her options then," Andy said, in the same sceptical tone of voice.

"What do you mean?" Luce asked her indignantly.

"I dunno, it just all seems too easy to me," said Andy. "The chances are that Tash'll find Peta's cut her knee, and she's in great danger of dripping blood all over the carpet, but Tash will rush and get a plaster, and save her mum from having to go mad because of the stain on the carpet."

In a way I was glad that Andy was putting forward the case for not believing it at all, because if I got really worried about anything I'd been told, I could just keep remembering how Andy found it so unbelievable. It had shocked me because most of it was unexpectedly brutal and not at all romantic. I knew it would be a long time before I'd lose the image of those all-seeing eyes.

"What else?" demanded Luce.

"A little animal that I'm going to try and rescue."

"What kind of an animal?"

"She didn't say."

"What a surprise." This last comment, as you probably guessed, was from Andy, who was getting more and more sarcastic by the minute. I decided to say something positive for a change.

"Oh, and something I'm doing really well ... at school, I think. A woman is going to be really pleased with me apparently, and I'm going to be a great success in the future."

"I could have told you that," Fen said, tucking her arm through mine. "Was that all?" she added.

I nearly didn't tell them about the blond boy-friend, but then I thought, why not? It'd certainly interest Luce! "Oh, and she said there was a tall, blond boy, older than me, about to appear..."

"And hey presto, here he is!" said Andy, in her most cynical tone yet. We all turned to where she was looking and there, strolling up to us, were Danny and Kim. It's true that Danny *is* tall and blond.

"Where were you?" I asked, feeling relieved at the sight of him, then immediately cross because he'd made Mum and me worry.

"Steve's," he replied in his usual brief way.

"Mum was really worried."

"I phoned her just after you'd left the house. She wasn't worried."

Suddenly realizing that my arm was in pain for the second time that day, I glanced down to see that once again Luce was clutching me in her claw-like grasp, while giving me a wide-eyed, stary look.

"So she was right, wasn't she?"

I tried to get my brain round what Luce was talking about. "Who?"

"Gypsy Tiramisu…"

"Tiramisu is the name of a creamy Italian dessert," Kim informed Luce.

"Gypsy thingy then. Don't split hairs. The point is that she told Tash a tall blond boy was about to appear, and a tall blond boy *has* appeared. So you see, Andy, it's *not* all rubbish. There *is* something in it."

"Believe it if you want," said Andy lightly, "but personally I'm going to have a go at the hoop-la stall over there. Anyone else coming?"

She strode off and we all followed, but no one spoke for a few minutes because I think we were all trying to work out what we felt about this fortune-telling business. Was there any truth in it? I didn't know, but I began to feel excited about going to school the next day and finding out which lesson I was going to excel in!

Typically, as the next day wore on, and not a single teacher praised me for anything in any lesson, the sense of wonder I'd felt after my fortune-telling session began to fade.

By the end of school, I think the others had really lost interest in the whole thing. Even Luce had stopped asking me for regular bulletins on how pleased or otherwise my teachers were with me.

Leah was on duty, but Luce, Jaimini and I were going to the café too. Andy and Fen were both needed for a sports practice of some sort so they couldn't come. As soon as we walked through the door I spotted that young man who had been there the previous day. He was on his own again. I wasn't the only one to spot him.

"Look, it's that professional athlete," whispered Luce, banging her fists against both Jaimini and me in her excitement. I happened to be looking at the man as Luce was saying that, and it was obvious that once again he was amused, and yet there was definitely no way he could have heard what Luce had whispered, and for once she wasn't making a fool of herself by staring at him or anything. He must have noticed my puzzled expression because he immediately started concentrating hard on stirring his tea.

It was Becky who took our order this time. Becky is in her early twenties and always speaks her mind, if you know what I mean. I think she likes us six, but hasn't got all that much in common with us, so we don't have a great deal of conversation with her. She doesn't joke with us like Mark and Kevin the chef, do. After a few minutes Leah appeared from the kitchen. She was looking quite despondent, I thought.

"I think Andy might be right, you know, Tash. I was just talking to Kevin and he's been telling me about this burst water main at the top of the High Street. He happened to say that he felt as though he was driving through a river when he came to work this morning, and I suddenly remembered what that gypsy said to you about the strange man who had something to do with water turning up in your life, and how Andy took the mickey and said it could be anyone. In a way she was right because, let's face it, it could have been Kevin."

"Yes, but Kevin hasn't brought trouble, has he?" asked Luce.

"Well, we don't know, do we? He may have done."

"I should stop looking for connections if I were you," said Jaimini sensibly. "Wait till something suddenly hits you as being spot on before you make judgements. If nothing particularly seems to connect, then maybe Andy's right."

"You're so sensible, aren't you, Jaimes?" Luce said warmly. Jaimini shot her a quick look to check she wasn't being sarcastic, but she wasn't, so I took Jaimini's advice and tried to get on with my life.

"Excuse me," said a man's voice, which gave us all a jump. It was the man who Luce thought was a professional athlete. We all gawped at him because we couldn't work out what on earth had brought him to our table. "I just thought you might like to know that actually I teach deaf and dumb children to lip-read."

With that he winked at Luce and strolled out of the café, leaving us sitting there gobsmacked. We were silent for at least ten seconds before all collapsing in giggles. Luce went bright red. "He obviously picked up our entire conversation," she said. "How embarrassing."

We laughed at Luce for a bit longer, then we all went off home, where the first of my connections happened.

"Hi, Mum, I'm back."

"Hi, Tash. I've got a surprise for you," she

replied as I walked through to the sitting room.

"What?"

It's amazing how quickly thoughts can whizz through your mind, isn't it? In the space of about three seconds at least five reasons why I was about to be surprised entered my head. Maybe a strange man, wearing wellies, was going to be in our sitting room, or perhaps I was going to find Peta with a cut knee, or our little dog Boo with a broken leg. Or would it be an entirely unconnected surprise, like new wallpaper or Danny with all his hair shaved off? The surprise wasn't any of these things.

Under the coffee table crouched the tiniest, most perfect little black kitten. But no sooner had I broken into a big beam of delight and said, "How sweet," than my delight evaporated and a great feeling of foreboding came over me. This must be the little animal that Gypsy Tirrasana had talked about. So it wasn't rubbish. Just wait till Andy heard about this.

"You don't look very pleased, Tash. What's the matter?"

"No, I am pleased, honestly. I was just remembering something else, that's all," I assured Mum as I slowly approached the sweet little thing, and Peta fixed me with her gravest expression.

"Ve kitten is called Scribble, Tash, 'cos it made me scribble when it walked on my drawing book, see, Tash. OK?" she explained in very serious tones.

"Scribble? Yeah, OK. But how come we've suddenly got a kitten, Mum, and where's Boo?"

"Danny's taken Boo out for a walk, and the reason we've got a kitten is because I'm such a soft touch. Old Mr Sadler's cat had five kittens, and I took one of them because I felt sorry for the poor man as he wasn't having much luck finding homes for them."

"And Scribble is a boy, see, Tash, because he's got a willy, see, Tash."

"Yes, Peta, thanks for the biology lesson," I said patiently.

Scribble suddenly tore across the room and went into the kitchen. Naturally we all followed and watched the poor animal while it peed in the litter tray.

"Cats are so clever, aren't they?" Mum said. "They click on so quickly about keeping themselves clean and where they're supposed to go to the loo, and that sort of thing, don't they?"

"Ackshally Mummy, they call it going to ve litter tray, not going to ve loo, 'cos it's not a loo, is it, Mummy? Is it, Tash?"

Peta was certainly very excited and interested in our new pet, because she then went on to tell me how it would need its 'jections at the vet's and various other jumbled up pieces of information about worms and fleas. I held little Scribble in my hands, and tried hard to remember exactly what Gypsy Tirrasana had said about a small animal. Had she said that I would save it from danger, or that it would be in danger, or that I would *try* and save it from danger? I really couldn't remember, and it suddenly seemed very important to be sure of my facts.

"Mum, am I allowed to go the fair again? I wouldn't stay there for very long at all. It's just that Jaimini couldn't go last night and she doesn't want to go tonight on her own, and none of the others can go because they've got too much homework, but I got ahead with my homework in the lunch hour."

"You can go if you're sure you can fit it in," she answered, as I guessed she would because Mum is always very reasonable about things, and she trusts Danny and me to organize our lives properly and to be able to judge whether we ought to do things.

"Thanks, Mum. I'll phone Jaimini."

Half an hour later I was standing with Luce and Jaimini outside Gypsy Tirrasana's tent, feeling like a nervous wreck. I had slightly bent the truth about Jaimini not having anyone to go with, and I felt guilty about that, because Mum's so reasonable about everything that I bet she would have let me go anyway.

"You're mad, spending another three pounds

fifty, Tash," Jaimini said, shaking her head slowly and making me feel really juvenile.

"No, I think she's quite right," Luce argued. "If I was Tash I'd really want to be sure of my facts. After all, we're talking about a life and death situation here, Jaimes. Poor little kitten. Surely a kitten's life is worth more than three pounds fifty, isn't it?"

"I don't know what you're on about," was Jaimini's dry response.

"Well, I know I'm mad, but I'm going anyway, because otherwise I'll only worry that I should have gone," I said quickly, before they started arguing.

"Good luck, Tash," they said, at exactly the same moment as I went in, my legs trembling.

The same man was in the outer tent, and I had to wait for about two minutes again. Then the same little bell told me to go in, but I got a shock to see it was green smoke this time and I found myself wondering if they had one colour for each day of the week. The glistening flashes of silver from the shimmer balls looked even more effective through the misty green haze. I wanted to hurry to get to the table with the crystal ball but I couldn't because it was impossible to see more in the dim candlelight.

"Come and sit down," came a voice out of the depths of the tent. Instead of encouraging me, though, the voice made me hesitate, because surely this wasn't the same voice as the previous day? It was low and raspy, but I didn't think it was the same. I approached cautiously, my eyes practically squinting with the effort of trying to see the person at the table.

I had thought that the moment I actually sat down, I would know immediately if this was the same woman, yet it was impossible to tell. The hair was shiny and black and curly, the yashmak covered the face, the dress was exactly the same, so were the earrings, even the fingerless gloves. I must have been imagining things when I heard the voice, because this *had* to be Gypsy Tirrasana.

"Let me see your palms."

Was that the same voice? The only difference was that yesterday the voice had been somehow breathier, but maybe she'd had a bad throat or something the previous day. After all, just because you told fortunes didn't mean you never had anything the matter with you.

I held out my palms, but she was looking at my face.

"Did I ... didn't I see you yesterday?"

I nodded.

"Nothing has changed since yesterday, I'm afraid. I can tell you nothing more. You can have your money refunded, of course."

Now I had to speak.

"It's all right. I just wanted to ask about the little animal that you mentioned?"

She turned to the crystal ball and spread her hands over it before gazing into it.

"Yes, the very small creature. It may be a cat or a dog. I think it is a domestic animal … yes, a cat."

"Am I going to manage to save it from the danger that you mentioned?"

She frowned and looked more closely at the ball for an awfully long time.

"Yes … but only just."

I felt relief flooding through me.

She turned back and I realized that she was waiting to see if I had any other little matters I wanted clearing up.

"Um, could you tell me some more about the man you mentioned?"

Again her eyes returned to the ball. "The man is, I think, blond…"

"Oh, the older boy, you mean?"

"Yes, the older boy … and he is tall…"

"Yes … um, is it a boyfriend exactly?" I asked very hesitantly.

"A boyfriend … yes. He has been watching you for some time. He is waiting for his moment to talk to you. He will be good for you and bring happiness into your life… Let me see your palms again." She studied them for ages. "Yes … you are kind and gentle and caring. Sometimes you feel guilty about things… And at the moment you have no boyfriend. Am I right?"

I wasn't sure if she was asking me if she was right about the lack of boyfriend or about the whole lot, but anyway I didn't want to give away any more about myself, so I just nodded. She could take that as she wanted.

"I thought so … no boyfriend … but there will be one soon … this tall boy, blond."

After that she spent ages just staring into the ball and staring at my palms alternately. It crossed my mind that maybe she had exhausted herself telling me so much about myself. As she stared at her ball, I thought hard about what she'd just said.

Was I kind? Yes, I supposed I was. Was I gentle and caring? Yes, I was, really. Did I sometimes feel guilty about things? Yes, that was definitely true. But she hadn't mentioned the little child. Maybe I ought to prompt her. No, that would make it too easy for her. On the other hand, she wouldn't bother to repeat herself unless I specifically asked her to.

"Um … the little child…"

"Yes, he is here."

"It's a boy then?"

"Yes, it's a boy."

"And how will I know when the danger is going to happen?"

"You will know as soon as you will know. That

is all I can say. If we knew when danger was about to come, the world would be a safer place, wouldn't it? Do you know a little boy?"

I thought about this. The only little boy I really knew was Andy's little brother, Sebastien. He was only just one, hardly more than a baby.

I nodded.

"Anything else…"

"Um … the strange man who's got something to do with water."

"Yes," she answered, looking at her crystal ball, "he comes from across water. And you must be careful…"

I waited, but that seemed to be it. What a disappointment. It had been a waste of time and money coming back. Even the atmosphere didn't feel the same as the previous day. If only I'd just left things alone.

"Thank you," I said, as I stood up, then I suddenly noticed something. Gypsy Tirrasana had painted her nails. They looked as I had expected them to look the previous day. The nail varnish was glittery metallic green. I glanced at her face, then back to her nails. But even though I'd only looked away for a second, when I looked back to her hands they were clasped together so I couldn't see the nails at all.

Chapter 3

This time, as I went out I didn't even notice if there was a man in the outer tent or not, I was so deep in my thoughts.

"What did she say? What did she say?" Luce cried, swooping down on me.

"She mentioned the same things again – the little animal, the little child – apparently it's a boy … Oh, and the blond boyfriend."

"The boyfriend!" Luce burst out. "You never told us she said anything about a boyfriend last time."

"No, she said it was a tall, blond, older boy…"

"Yes, and Danny appeared straight after."

"Yes, only today she said it was a boyfriend. She even asked me if I'd got a boyfriend, so perhaps it was nothing to do with Danny at all."

"I shouldn't get your hopes up," Jaimini said gently.

"Oh, shut up, Jaimes, you're as bad as Andy."

Jaimini ignored that. "What else did she say?"

"She said I was kind and gentle and caring and sometimes felt guilty about things."

Luce positively gasped then. "And she's got that absolutely spot on, hasn't she? Come on, Jaimes, you can't deny that that is a hundred per cent accurate."

"Yes, I know, but if I was sitting looking at Tash with her big worried eyes, I could say those things too, and be pretty sure I was going to hit the nail on the head."

"Did she mention the stranger?"

"Only that he would arrive from across water."

"Uh-oh, here comes the tall blond boy again," said Luce.

She was grinning and I turned to follow her gaze. Sure enough, Danny was approaching me. I couldn't believe it. I mean, once was a coincidence, but twice, that was too much. Unless Danny wasn't the tall blond boy at all, and I really was about to have a boyfriend. That would be good!

"Tash, you've got to go home quickly!"

"Why? What's happened?"

"The kitten's gone missing. Mum think it's got outside because she's searched the whole house. I've got to go to football training, and Mum can't leave Peta."

"I'll see you tomorrow," I called to Luce and Jaimini as I went tearing off, following Danny who ran with big, slow, easy strides and no effort.

My heart was thumping away, partly because of trying to keep up with Danny and partly because however much Jaimini and Andy and loads of other people didn't believe in fortune-telling at all, there was no denying that I was rushing home because a tiny cat was in danger.

"It's all right. Panic over. Sorry to drag you away," were Mum's first words as Danny and I crashed into the house.

"Where was he?" I asked, spotting Scribble chasing a little felt mouse behind the settee.

"He'd somehow managed to get round the back of the fridge," Mum explained, as Danny grabbed his kitbag and tore off to football training.

All the way home I had been imagining situations where I had to rescue Scribble, and in a way it was a bit of an anticlimax to come home and find that the drama was over. Peta was in bed too, so the place was even more peaceful.

I went up to my room and started revising for a biology test the next day, but just before I settled down to work, something caught my eye out of the window. Standing facing our house, about a hundred metres away, was a man. There was something about the way he was standing that was familiar, but I couldn't work out what it was. I kept my eyes on him and willed him to turn round. At one point he half turned, but it was so brief that I couldn't make out his face at all, then he walked away.

That night I dreamt that every lesson I went to in school there was a strange man sitting in the chair next to me, but when I tried to look at his face, it disappeared and there was only flesh where the eyes and the nose and everything should be. It was a terrifying dream and I woke up with a start and sat up in bed feeling scared to go back to sleep again in case I carried on with the same dream.

It was as I was going through the dream in my head that I realized that Gypsy Tirrasana hadn't said anything more about me doing well in school. The previous day she'd mentioned how a woman was going to be pleased with me and praise me. I suddenly felt really despondent, because that had been the only good bit of that reading, and the second one didn't have anything good in it (apart from the boyfriend bit, of course).

I looked at my watch. Ten past three in the morning. It was the next day already. Maybe I'd go back and see the gypsy again, only this time I'd go in disguise. Yes, that was it. That was what I would do. It took me ages to get back to sleep because I was so excited about my latest plan and I was working out all the different disguises I could use.

The following morning break at school found us all down at the netball courts, our favourite outdoor meeting place. Nobody ever went down to the courts at break times, and even though the staffroom looked out over them, it was too far away for the staff to hear what we were saying or anything.

"Tell the others what the gypsy told you yesterday," Luce instructed me in her usual un-thinking way. I hadn't actually planned on telling the others, except Fen, because I didn't want to hear Andy's cynical viewpoint, *or* Jaimini's.

"Oh, it was nothing much different from the previous day," I said as breezily as I could, but Luce had got everyone interested, so I had to say something. "She just said more or less the same thing…"

"No, she didn't," Luce interrupted. "And tell them what the surprise was your mum had for you, Tash."

I opened my mouth to speak, but Luce was already launching in on my behalf.

"A kitten. A little black kitten. So that proves it, Andy."

"Proves what?" asked Andy, calmly.

"Proves it's not all rubbish," replied Luce,

"because Gypsy Tiramisu…"

"Tirrasana!" everybody corrected her loudly.

"Yeah – thingy – said that Tash would save a little animal from danger and now she's got one to save, hasn't she?"

Luce was grinning round triumphantly, and the rest of us were looking at Andy to see what she had to say to that.

"I thought she'd already got one," came Andy's irritatingly calm answer.

"What?"

"The puppy, Boo," replied Andy.

"Yes, I know, but Boo's bigger than the kitten," Luce said, sounding quite moody.

"So what?" said Andy.

"So… Oh, I don't know!" Luce answered, rather snappily. "Say something, Tash. I'm doing all the work here," she added crossly.

"Well, if you don't believe in predictions, you don't believe in them and that's that," I said. "The thing is, I can't stop thinking about it. I keep thinking that something's going to happen to Peta. After all, Peta does sound as though she's a boy, doesn't she?"

"Oh, it's a boy who's in danger as well as a little animal, is it?" asked Andy.

"Leave Tash alone," said Fen.

"Sorry, Tash. I can't help it," Andy said, with a grin.

"I'm sure you're right, but it doesn't stop me thinking about things. She actually said it was a cat as well, and it does seem to be a bit of a coincidence that until yesterday we didn't even have a kitten."

"You're not kidding," Luce said. "Sounds spooky to me."

"That would be a good name for a kitten actually," Fen said dreamily.

"Peta's named it Scribble."

"How come your mum decided to get a kitten?" Jaimini asked. So I explained where Mum had got Scribble from. I'd already told Fen, but none of the others knew. Then we talked a bit more about Gypsy Tirrasana, though I'd long since decided not to say anything about how I was going to go back a third time and have my fortune told. I thought they'd think I was really stupid. I even thought I was stupid myself, because I couldn't afford yet another three pounds fifty. I'd have to borrow the money from Danny.

"Why don't you go back again tonight?" Luce suggested, just as though she could read my mind, eyes twinkling like mad. Leah and Fen looked as though they thought it was a good idea but they didn't like to say so. Jaimini and Andy, on the other hand both immediately said, "No, don't, Tash," and "That's a stupid idea, Luce."

"I know! Why don't *I* go instead?" Luce then

proposed. "I'll look very soft and sweet like Tash, and see if she says the same things as she said to Tash. That'll be much more interesting."

"Yeah, that's a good idea," Fen agreed. "That'll save Tash some money."

"I'm not doing it to save Tash some money," said Luce, "I'm doing it to try to prove to Andy and Jaimes that there *is* something in all this, even though they don't think so."

"Go ahead," said Jaimini. "I don't mind."

It was my turn to work after school, so I went in through the back door straight into the kitchen, while the others went in through the main door.

"Hiya, Tash," said Kevin.

"Hiya, Kevin."

Kevin the chef is really nice. He's twenty-something, small, dark and very strong. Jan thinks he's an excellent chef. He's an interesting person, because you could easily get the impression that he's not paying attention to anything except the cooking he's doing, but in actual fact he's aware of an awful lot more than we think. He's got a great sense of humour and never wastes words.

When I'd worked in the kitchen for about twenty minutes I went through to the café to make some drinks, and as usual had a quick glance round to see if there was anyone I knew in there, apart from my friends, of course. I immediately spotted the woman we'd seen on the Monday. If anything, she looked even gaudier this time. She was wearing a huge swirling Indian dress, with lots of dangly bits. Her face was heavy with make-up again and she wore the same big scarf.

Fen was gesticulating wildly that she wanted another drink so I went over to ask her what she wanted.

"Have you seen who's over there?" she whispered to me.

I nodded. "She looks really weird."

"She's staring at you, Tash."

I didn't reply because Jan had appeared right behind me and heard what Fen said.

"Just ignore that woman, Tash," Jan said, seriously. "I'll deal with her. I've already had to have words with her, I'm afraid."

"What about?" asked Luce, ever the subtle one.

"That's between me and her," replied Jan, looking none too pleased.

All the same I couldn't help glancing over in her direction every so often, and whenever I did, she seemed to be staring back at me, but then she quickly averted her eyes when she saw me looking.

"Come on, let's go straight to the fair right now," Luce said, trying to drink non-existent lemonade from her glass.

"Count me out," said Jaimini. "I've got too much homework."

"Me too," said Andy, though it was obvious Andy was only not going because she thought the whole thing was stupid.

"I've got to practise my violin," said Leah, looking really apologetic. "I've hardly done a thing and it's my lesson tomorrow."

"I'll come with you," Fen said, probably because she felt sorry for Luce.

"Give me a ring tonight to tell me what happens," I said to Luce.

So off they all went and right up till six o'clock when I finished work, I kept wondering how Luce was getting on.

It was as I was leaving the café that I caught sight of that same man again, the one I'd seen from my bedroom window. He was walking up the High Street and I found myself following him and trying to catch up. He must have been speeding up because the gap between us began to grow wider, then just when I was thinking of giving up, he suddenly turned round and I got the shock of my life! It was my dad! I hadn't seen Dad for two years, but I knew it was definitely him.

"Dad!" I yelled at the top of my voice, and at least four people turned to see who was shouting in the street like that. Dad turned away, though, and began that rapid walking again. I didn't know what to think. Had he heard me? He *must* have done. Then why had he deliberately walked away from me? And why hadn't he come and talked to me in the first place? I stood rooted to the spot, feeling utterly perplexed, and then very slowly another feeling began to come over me, and this was scary.

Gypsy Tirrasana had said that a man was about to appear in my life, unexpectedly. So this must be the man. My dad! I decided I'd go straight home and tell Mum. Then as I rushed home, half walking, half running, I began to have second thoughts about that. She'd said he would mean trouble and that I mustn't do anything. She must have meant that I would make the trouble worse if I did anything. Did that include telling Mum? Yes, it must do. Of course it would, because Mum would be upset if she knew that Dad was around.

Mum had tried to cover it up, but Danny and I both knew that she'd been really angry when Dad had moved so far away and the visits had stopped, then the phone calls too. I'd been cross at the time as well. First I'd been upset, then cross, then after a bit I'd just got used to it, and decided that if this was the way it was supposed to be, there was absolutely nothing I could do about it.

When I went into the house I spent ages talking to Mum, because I wanted plenty of time to

notice whether or not she was on edge, or showing any other signs of tension. There didn't
appear to be any. She couldn't have any idea that
Dad was around. Next I would try Danny. I
couldn't wait till he got back from school. As
usual he was late because he practically always
does something or other after school. He hardly
ever comes straight home.

At seven-thirty the phone rang. It was Luce.

"How did it go?" I asked.

"She wasn't there," she answered despondently.

"Why not?"

"Dunno. The tent was gone and everything. I
suppose even fortune-tellers have to have a day
off, don't they?"

When Luce said that, it suddenly made me feel
as though Andy was right and the whole thing
was completely stupid.

"I'm going to take Jaimini's advice and forget
about it all until something really does seem to be
coming true."

"Good idea. I'll see you tomorrow. Bye."

"Yeah, bye."

But something *had* come true, hadn't it? The
strange man had appeared in my life. I began to
wonder whether Dad would have had to cross a
river to come to Cableden. He lived so far away,
there was certain to be at least one river to cross
to come to this part of the world.

The next day at school we had PSE, which is the one lesson we all have together. All the best teachers seem to teach PSE or Personal and Social Education to give it its full title. We used to have Mrs Merle, who is now our music teacher, and now we have Mrs Gibson, who's almost as popular as Mrs Merle.

As soon as we walked into the classroom we could see it was going to be a really interesting lesson, because there was another woman standing at the front with Mrs Gibson. We'd been discussing all about how more and more hedges were being ripped out these days, and fences being put up in their place, and we'd talked about all the wildlife that lived in the hedgerows. It turned out that this lady – Mrs Turner – was a hedgerow specialist. She was so keen on wildlife that she attracted all sorts of birds into her garden by keeping weird and wonderful bird-tables, bird-houses and even bird-baths. She was also a bee-keeper.

We all listened with fascination – at least *I* did – to Mrs Gibson's bee stories, then we watched a short film about them. She explained exactly how bees all work together to make the honey. I love learning about things like that. I'm a bit like Mum, I suppose. She loves the outdoor life and she's always been interested in wildlife in general. I asked loads of questions, and you know how you can just tell when a teacher or a grown-up likes you? Well, I had the feeling that Mrs Turner appreciated all my questions.

When the bell went I was really hacked off. The last thing I felt like doing was going to French, because there were still loads of things I wanted to ask Mrs Turner about. As everybody else piled out of the room, I went to the front and asked if it was true that bees do a sort of dance that's all carefully worked out.

"Yes it is, and I was going to go on to explain all about that, but unfortunately we ran out of time," Mrs Turner smiled.

"And have you got any film of a bird getting food from your complicated bird table?" I then asked.

"No, but that's next on my list of things to do," she replied.

"Can Mrs Turner come back next week to carry on?" I asked Mrs Gibson, and the two women exchanged looks which clearly said, "Unfortunately, that's just not possible."

"I'm afraid ... um, sorry, what *is* your name?"

"Tash. Tash Johnston."

"And is there any particular reason for your interest in bees and so on?" Mrs Turner then asked me.

"No, not really. I just love everything that you were talking about. My mum's like that, too."

Mrs Turner gave me a huge smile then, as though I'd given her the very answer she was looking for.

"Would you be interested to see the bird-tables and the bees, Tash?"

"Yes, I really would," I answered, trying not to sound too much like a silly little girl with a big craze on bees.

"Well, my phone number is in the book. The house is called Brooksby. Ask your mum to give me a ring, and if you want to pop down to my place and have a look, that would be fine. I should keep it to yourself, though. I don't want the whole of Cableden Comprehensive thinking along the same lines. It's just that I can tell you are a genuine enthusiast."

"Oh, thank you very much," I said, and was rewarded by big beams from Mrs Turner *and* Mrs Gibson.

Even better than that, I'd managed to miss at least five minutes of French with the perfect excuse that Mrs Gibson kept me behind to talk.

After school, Fen and I walked down to the café on our own. Jaimini had gone on ahead with Leah and Andy, and Luce had gone belting off to the fair, even though the rest of us had tried to tell her that it was only on for three days and it would have gone by now.

"You know what suddenly occurred to me?"

said Fen, thoughtfully.

"What?"

"Mrs Turner really liked you, didn't she?"

"I think so."

"And she was obviously really pleased with you, wasn't she?"

"Yes, I reckon."

"Well, there you are then. Don't you see?"

"No. What?"

"It's another thing that's come true."

"What…?" I stopped in my tracks as I clicked on to what Fen was getting at. "Yes, you're right. And something else happened to me yesterday," I said hesitantly.

"What?" Fen asked, turning big eager eyes on me. I hadn't been going to tell anyone about seeing my dad, because it was too personal in a way, but now I decided I would, because I couldn't tell Mum, and I wasn't even sure if it would be a good idea to tell Danny, yet I was dying to tell someone.

"I saw my dad."

"What!"

"When I'd finished work yesterday, he was walking up the High Street. I didn't realize it was him at first, but something made me follow him, then he turned and I recognized him and I called out, but he turned back quickly and hurried off."

"Oh Tash, that's terrible. Why didn't he stop when he heard you call?"

"I don't know. I don't even know if he *did* hear me call."

"Have you told your mum?"

"I daren't."

"But surely your mum would know if he was here in Cableden?"

"Not necessarily."

"Maybe he's here to… Oh no, it's OK."

Fen suddenly looked really embarrassed.

"What, Fen?"

"Nothing. It was a stupid idea. Forget it."

"Oh, please tell me!"

"Well, you know how you hear about divorced parents where one parent has got custody…"

"You mean, maybe he's here to try and snatch us away from Mum?"

"I'm sure he couldn't be. I don't know why I even thought it."

"Yes, but you could be right, Fen. I'm going to warn Danny – and Mum."

"No, you'll only upset your mum. I'm probably just being dramatic. Maybe just tell Danny."

"Look!" I exclaimed, grabbing Fen's arm.

There, just coming out of the café about fifty metres ahead, was my dad.

Chapter 4

"That's him. That's Dad!" I said, in a shaky voice.

"Don't let him see you, Tash," said Fen, pulling me into the entrance of a shop. "This is serious," she added, "because of Peta."

"What do you mean, because of Peta?"

"He might try to snatch Peta."

"Oh Fen, maybe that's another prediction that's going to come true! Gypsy Tirrasana said that a little child was in danger. Maybe the stranger and the trouble and the little child in danger are all tied up together!"

"You've *got* to tell your mum, Tash."

"I daren't, Fen. The gypsy said I mustn't do anything. I must just wait. I got the impression I'd make things worse if I even did something little like tell Mum."

"Why don't you tell Danny then?"

"Yes, I was thinking about that."

"You don't *want* to live with your dad, do you, Tash?"

"No, of course not. I want to stay with Mum. I want to stay here in Cableden with you lot."

"Oh, good. Just checking."

Inside the café we sat down with Leah and Fen, but didn't say anything about my dad. After a while, Luce came pelting in, looking ready to burst.

When she'd caught her breath, she told us what had happened. "The fair was all packed up when I got there, but I spoke to someone or other who said that Gypsy Tiramisu wasn't anything to do with the fair, but was a local person who nobody ever saw except when she was doing readings. I didn't believe this, so I asked someone else connected with the fair, who said of course Gypsy Tiramisu was a real gypsy, and that she would be travelling with the rest of them. So then I searched everywhere to try to find the gypsy, but I couldn't find her anywhere, so I asked *someone else*, and they told me that most of the lorries and caravans had left ages ago. So I decided to give up and come back here."

I looked at Luce's flushed face and said slowly, "So, if the *first* person you spoke to is right, maybe I *will* get to see Gypsy Tirrasana again..."

All the way home I couldn't stop thinking

about what Luce had said. I'd always thought that fortune-tellers travelled around all the time. I found it really difficult to believe in one who just lived in a normal house, like normal people. On the other hand, the other person had said that that wasn't true. When I'd really quizzed Luce about this, she insisted that both people she'd spoken to had been part of the fair. They'd both been men, and they'd both sounded very sure about what they were saying.

As soon as Mum was safely occupied giving Peta a bath, I tapped gently on Danny's door. I knew he was in his room doing homework.

"Yeah," came the usual answer.

"Can I come in for a sec, Danny?"

"'K."

Danny never wastes words. He was sitting at his computer. On the screen was a poster for something.

"That looks brilliant, Dan."

"Can't get the frame right."

"Well, it's no use me offering any advice because I wouldn't have a clue."

"'S easy. Here."

He stood up and indicated that I should hold the mouse and get on with it. He was giving me a sort of lesson.

"Right, what frame d'you want?" He showed me a sheet of paper with all the choices, and I pointed to one, feeling totally unenthusiastic, because all I wanted to do was talk about Dad. On the other hand I knew the importance of having Danny in a good mood for this conversation, so I couldn't afford to rile him by refusing to have a go at the simplest thing on his computer.

"Yeah, press that..." he was saying. "Yeah, enter... Move that mouse up there ... yeah ... the second one. God, Tash, hadn't you realized we'd actually entered the age of technology? Where have you been for the past five years?"

"Sorry, Dan. I've never taken to computers."

"Well, you do IT at school, don't you? How do you manage?"

"As best I can."

"OK, I'll do it."

I jumped up quickly and he sat back down again and changed the screen about ten times in two seconds to get back to where he was.

"I wanted to tell you something, Dan."

"What?"

"It's quite an important thing. Well, you might know about it already. But if you don't, it's important."

"Go on." He was concentrating on the screen and not on me, but I had no choice. I had to go for it.

"I saw Dad today ... and also yesterday."

Danny didn't appear to react at all, but then I

saw that the knuckles had gone white on the hand that clutched the mouse. My heart seemed to be gradually getting a bit too loud for the room.

"You can't have done." Still he didn't turn round, and the images on the screen were changing again.

"Well, I did."

"Where?"

"Outside the café at about four o'clock today. And yesterday I followed him up the High Street. I wasn't sure who it was at first…"

"What! You followed a strange man, not knowing who it was? You're mad!"

I could hardly throw in that a gypsy at the fair had predicted that a man would be coming into my life and bringing trouble, could I? It suddenly seemed completely stupid in the presence of Danny.

"I *did* recognize him, and something just sort of made me follow him, then when he turned round I suddenly realized it was Dad and I called out to him, and he heard me – I'm sure he did – but he turned back round again and walked away."

At this point Danny swung round on his stool. "How far away were you?"

"About fifty metres."

"You could have easily been mistaken then."

"I'm sure it was him."

"Are you certain he heard you?"

"Not a hundred per cent certain."

"Oh God, Tash."

"Ninety-nine per cent, though."

"Right, let's test your theory, shall we?"

He jumped up and tore past me out of the bedroom. About ten seconds later he was back with the phone. From one of his drawers he pulled out a tatty little book, flipped the pages hard, then began punching numbers into the phone. My heart was definitely too loud for this room.

"That proves it," he said, as he shoved the aerial back in the phone, put it on his desk and turned to his computer.

"What?" I asked in a little cracked voice, because this aggressive Danny always makes me feel scared. Danny is only ever like this when anything to do with Mum, Dad, divorce or new partners comes up. The rest of the time he is easygoing and lovely, but he can't handle this relationships thing. Goodness knows how Kim puts up with him.

"That was Dad who answered the phone just then. So he can hardly have made a hundred and sixty-odd mile journey since four o'clock, can he?"

"It can't have been Dad."

"It was."

"Oh." There was nothing more to be said. I

sidled out of his room and went into the bathroom because I suddenly wanted to be in a nice comfortable room. The bathroom was full of steam and bubbles and happiness. Mum and Peta were laughing away. I watched for a moment before they realized I was there. This was Peta at her very sweetest.

"Gen," said Peta. "Dooota gen, Mummy."

Mum held this big yellow duck under the water and put on a really funny voice, pretending to be the duck. "I'm searching for my dinner. Oh deary, deary me, where is my dinner? I want a nice juicy fish…" Then Mum suddenly let out a shriek as presumably the duck touched Peta's toe (I couldn't see because of all the bubbles), then she let the duck go and it shot out of the water and immediately bobbed back on the surface again, which made Peta laugh and laugh with such innocent, infectious laughter, that I found myself laughing, too.

"Hello, Tasha," she said, putting her little chubby arms up for me to give her a kiss. I didn't mind that she was all wet. I bent forward and she covered me in kisses while practically strangling me. "Oh, hello, Danny," she said into my hair. "All ve family is in ve bafroom now!"

"I'm going round to Kim's, Mum. I won't be long," Danny said.

"See you later, then." Mum smiled at him

through the steam. I was looking at Mum not Danny, but when I became aware that he was still standing there a few seconds later I *did* look at him.

"Sorry," he mouthed to me with a half-smile.

I nodded with the same nearly smile. Danny is so nice, really. It's just frustrating that I can never, *ever* discuss anything to do with Mum or Dad with him. I went out of the bathroom on the third game of flying ducks, and on an impulse went back into Danny's room. He'd put his notebook back in the drawer, but I took it out and carefully found Dad's number, and tapped it into the phone. My heart was in my mouth but I had to do this. I got the shock of my life when a woman's voice answered.

"Hello?"

"Hello. Could I speak to Don Johnston, please?"

"I'm afraid he doesn't live here any more. Would you like me to give you his new number?"

"Yes, please … um, has he moved far away?"

"No, just to the next village."

"Oh, right."

I scribbled the number on the corner of the back page in the notebook and hoped that Danny wouldn't see it, but there was nothing else handy to write on. Then I thanked the woman and rang off. So the man's voice that Danny had heard had not been Dad's. It took me quite a few minutes to get my courage together to tap in this new number, but eventually I did because I realized that Mum and Peta would be out of the bathroom any minute.

After fourteen rings I gave up, and half of me felt relieved, but the other half felt more anxious than ever because if there was no reply, that was because I was right. I *had* seen Dad in Cableden. Fen's words came back to me. What if he *was* here to try and take Peta? The following day was Friday. I'd skip school. I'd lie in wait at the nursery school that Peta goes to on Fridays. Mum works at this holiday complex, you see. The rest of the week she works from home, but on Fridays she always spends the day at the complex.

My imagination began to take over. That was it! Dad had spent the last couple of days finding out about our family and our movements, and now he'd sussed that Mum worked out of the house on Fridays, he would be lying in wait for little Peta. I went in my room and sat on my bed frowning with concentration.

I absolutely hated all this. I couldn't bear it. The gypsy was right. This was trouble, all right. I'd never be able to handle it on my own. What would I do if he went into the nursery school? Would I march in after him and right when he was in the middle of telling the supervisor that he was Peta's dad and that he'd come to take her home, would I leap to the rescue and protest loudly that he was kidnapping my little sister? No, it was no good. I would be no more capable of leaping to the rescue than I would of leaping to the moon. I needed advice, so I phoned Fen.

When I'd finished explaining everything to her, Fen asked me if I wanted someone with me, patrolling the nursery school the next day. I said I knew it was crazy, but that I just didn't think I'd be able to handle it on my own. She said that she thought that I ought to ask Andy, as she was the daring one, and she'd probably see it as a challenge.

"I can't ask Andy, Fen. She already thinks I'm pathetic for believing a gypsy at a fair."

"Yes, but this is different. You really *have* seen your dad, haven't you?"

"Well, Danny doesn't think so."

"Yes, I know, but you *know* so, don't you?"

"Yes, I think so."

"But do you *know* so?" Fen insisted.

"I was completely sure until Danny was so dismissive."

"But he was only dismissive because he thought he heard your dad's voice on the phone, only he was wrong, wasn't he?"

"Yes, but he was dismissive before that as well."

"Well, no wonder. I mean, it's a very hard thing

to believe, isn't it, unless you actually saw your dad with your own eyes. And you *did*, didn't you?"

"Yes, I think so."

We were back to square one. Fen sighed. "Andy definitely won't come unless you sound convincing, you know," she pointed out, patiently.

"But what if we go to Peta's nursery school and sit there all day and nothing happens?"

"You'll have to warn Andy that that could easily happen. Tell you what, Tash, if Andy won't come, *I* will, OK?"

I was on the point of asking her why she didn't just come in the first place when she said, "I'd come anyway, but we all know that Andy is much better in these situations."

"I'll try and phone her right away, and I'll ring you back."

So we rang off and I phoned Andy. Her mum answered in her strong French accent that I love, and said she'd go and get Andy.

"Hi, Tash."

"Hi. I've got something to tell you and something to ask you. And you might think it's stupid and you might not, but I've decided to go for it anyway."

"Yeah?"

Andy was like Danny in some ways. She didn't say unnecessary things, especially not on the phone. I wished I could see her face and then I would know how she was reacting as I went through the whole thing that I'd only just gone through with Fen. At the end there was silence. It crossed my mind that she might have got bored and rung off ages ago.

"Andy?"

"Yeah ... sounds interesting ... and I fancy a day off school."

"So you'll come?"

"Yeah. What are you going to have?"

"What do you mean?"

"What illness? What excuse for missing school? We don't want the same thing wrong with us."

"Really bad cold. I'll do the note on Monday."

"OK, I'll have stomach upset. Where shall we meet?"

The meeting place was fairly crucial because we had to make sure we actually saw Peta being dropped off at nursery school and going safely inside. On the other hand, we mustn't let Mum see us. I had to leave the house as though I was going off for a normal day at school and so did Andy; then we planned to meet at the top of this little alleyway, from where we'd be able to see Mum draw up outside the nursery school in her car. We agreed to meet at ten-to-nine. Mum would arrive a few minutes later.

I phoned Fen to tell her what I'd arranged with Andy, and she was really pleased for me and wished me lots of luck. We said we'd risk going to the café afterwards because teachers hardly ever went there, and the chances of one of the very teachers that actually taught Andy or me on Fridays turning up were very small.

So the following morning I went off to school with my bag. As soon as I was out of sight, I began running. It was quite a roundabout route I had to take to get to the nursery school. It would have been a lot easier if I could have turned left outside our front gate, but I couldn't, because that wasn't the way to school and I couldn't be absolutely certain that Mum wasn't looking out of a window at that moment.

Andy was already there when I got to the alley-way. She wasn't wearing her school uniform. She was wearing skin-tight jeans, a black top and trainers, and she looked absolutely minute. She's the smallest in our group, but in school uniform she never looked quite as small as this.

"How did you get away without uniform?" I asked her, suddenly feeling very conspicuous.

"Dad's in France and I told Mum it was non-uniform day," she explained lightly, her eyes never leaving the road, and frequently flicking to left or right.

She's so quick thinking. I would never have thought of that. That's the difference between us. I knew exactly what she meant about her dad being in France, though, because although nothing in the world seems to scare Andy, there *is* one thing that does, and that's her dad. She loves her mum but she seems to be able to more or less wind her round her little finger. Her mum would never dream of checking up about the non-uniform day, for example, whereas her dad, if he suspected anything, definitely would.

"There's your mum," Andy announced calmly. Instinctively I pressed myself back against the hedge at the side of the alleyway. Andy stayed where she was and a few minutes later said, "Right, now we know that Peta is safely in there, because your mum's getting back into her car."

As Mum drove off, I unpeeled myself from the hedge. Slowly, Andy and I realized what a boring day this was going to be. By twenty-past nine all the mothers had dropped off their children and I began to feel not only bored but starving hungry.

"Do you want me to go and get some sweets from Meads?" Andy offered, brightly.

"No, I don't want to be left here on my own," I said quickly.

"Well, *you* go then," Andy said, then immediately changed her mind. "No, we need you here, don't we, to identify your dad."

"I'll just have to be hungry," I replied, as my stomach did a huge protesting rumble.

By ten o'clock we were going crazy with boredom but neither of us wanted to give up quite so soon. Andy surprised me then by asking me to tell her the gypsy story in detail. So I did. I also explained what Luce had said about the two different versions of who the gypsy actually was. As I was talking I could tell Andy was interested, and that made me stop worrying and just get on with the story. By the time I'd finished I got the feeling that she'd almost changed her mind and maybe she thought, like me, that there could be something in it.

"I wouldn't mind trying to find her," she said, softly.

"Who?"

"The one who lives locally."

I frowned and weighed up her words. Slowly, I was realizing what Andy thought.

"So ... you think ... that there are two gypsies?" I asked, tentatively.

"I think there's one gypsy who couldn't tell a fortune from a foxglove, and I think there's another woman who lives round here somewhere and who may not be a complete fraud."

This was something I'd never considered, and I couldn't consider it then either, because something unexpected happened. Out of the nursery school came a little trail of tiny children. They were all dressed up in their coats and holding hands with a partner and there were three adults with them.

"They're going on a walk," Andy whispered.

"Can you see Peta?" I whispered back, as I pressed myself back into the hedge.

"Yes, she's holding hands with a boy."

"What shall we do?"

"Follow them, of course. This is much more fun. They might even be going past Meads."

How could Andy be so casual about it? Personally, my knees were knocking. The line of children set off at a snail's pace with one adult in front, one at the back and one roughly halfway. There were eighteen children. Because the pace was so incredibly slow there was no way Andy and I could leave our hiding place until they'd gone quite a way, because the woman at the front of the line kept on turning round to see how the children behind her were getting on. She would be sure to spot Andy and me, and then she'd wonder why we hadn't overtaken, so we had no choice but to remain hidden. As there weren't that many hiding places, we had to watch them like hawks until they were practically out of sight, then belt out of our alleyway and run like mad till we found another suitable place to dive into.

"This doesn't look good," Andy said, biting her lip and looking round. "We're drawing far too much attention to ourselves like this. We're approaching that little section of shops. I'm going to walk completely normally and overtake them, then go into a shop and keep watch till they've gone past, then come out again and walk along quite slowly. They're probably going to the rec, aren't they, so I'll make my way there. You stay here till they're out of sight, then walk slowly towards the rec and I'll see you there."

It all sounded very straightforward, yet I was petrified of leaving Andy's side. Pathetic, isn't it?

"OK then ... where shall we meet on the rec?"

"I'll find *you*, don't worry."

She gave me a bright smile, presumably thinking that that would stop me worrying, then off she sauntered. I wished I was like Andy. I saw her go into the shop and I watched her come out again. At least I think it was her. The little line of three-year-old dots was steadily making its way to the rec, so I came out of hiding and began to follow as slowly as I could without looking suspicious. I felt self-conscious in my school uniform and hoped that there wasn't some very public-spirited person watching me through their window, about to go and dob on me to the head of our school.

I felt all panicky as it suddenly occurred to me that Peta might spot Andy. Oh no, Andy obviously hadn't thought about that! I was going past the sweet shop – Meads – and decided to look in the shop window. In fact, it might be an idea to look in all the shop windows along there. That would give the nursery school outing enough time to get to the rec, then I could start tailing them again without going at minus two miles an hour.

It was as I was looking in the window of the estate agent's next door to the sweet shop that I nearly had a heart attack, because, reflected in the glass, I could clearly see that there was a man standing behind me, and though the reflection was blurred, I was sure it was my dad.

Chapter 5

I felt as though my knees were about to buckle and I was going to slither down on to the pavement. My eyes seemed so wide it was a wonder that they weren't boring a hole in the window. I thought that if I stayed perfectly still he might just disappear. I saw him take a step closer to me and though I wanted to cry out I kept myself as still as a statue, and the next second he moved away and went into the estate agent's!

So now I was staring at him through the window itself, rather than through the reflection in the window. He was walking round as though he owned the place, and a moment later I realized that he probably did. He had walked through to what must have been a private office at the back, followed by a woman who was presumably his secretary. By this time, my eyes were popping out of my head.

Dad worked here! That was impossible. He couldn't be working here right under Mum's nose like this. She would have said something. Or would she? Maybe Mum was perfectly happy with the arrangement? No, she couldn't possibly know. And anyway, why should Dad have any reason whatsoever for living so close to us if he didn't come and visit us? Unless... Yes, that *had* to be it. He was spending ages carefully following us all, to work out our routines. Obviously that kind of thing couldn't be done in a couple of days. He was being really thorough, so that when he chose his moment to snatch Peta, it would be the perfect operation.

I suddenly remembered that poor old Andy was somewhere on the rec, probably wondering where on earth I'd got to. I turned abruptly and ran over there as fast as I could, only slowing down when I'd spotted the nursery-school children playing around not far away.

"Tash, over here," came Andy's voice, from somewhere quite close by. I spotted her crouched down behind a litter bin, and went to join her.

"I've seen him," I gasped, because I was pretty puffed out.

"Where?"

"In the estate agent's. He's got an office there."

"What!" She was looking at me as though I'd definitely got several pages stuck together.

As soon as the words were out of my mouth I realized how stupid they sounded.

"I ... I saw him go into his office at the back," I said, blushing.

"How can your dad work in Cableden?" she asked, levelling her big brown eyes at me and giving me a sympathetic look, as though she was seriously considering having me committed.

"I don't know ... I don't understand it myself, but he was there."

"And you *are* certain it's your dad?"

"Well, I *was*."

"How long is it since you've actually seen your dad, Tash?"

"Um ... about two and a half years."

"Well, he's probably changed in that time, and also your view of him must have changed. You were only ten then."

"Yeah."

"Still at primary. You see things differently at primary."

"Yeah." I felt so stupid.

"Look, tell you what. We'll go back there together and I'll somehow work it so he has to come out of his office; then you can really get a good look at him."

"Andy, you can't!"

"Just watch me."

She got hold of my hand and began lugging me

back towards the estate agent's.

"I daren't," I kept saying.

"It's not you, it's me," she kept replying.

When we were right outside and looking in through the window, Andy told me her new plan.

"I've been thinking, we don't actually need to *see* the guy, we just need to know his name."

"What if he's changed it?"

"No, he won't have changed it. People don't usually change their names," was her glib answer. I wasn't too sure that I agreed with her on that, but Andy was in one of her no-nonsense-let's-get-on-with-it moods, so I knew there was no point in questioning her logic. She was on the point of striding into the estate agent's when my dad came out of the back office and, horror of horrors, appeared outside the door. I immediately turned my back to him, but before I knew it Andy's bright little voice had piped up, "Excuse me, I'm terribly sorry to trouble you, but my friend thinks she might know you."

I honestly thought I must have been dreaming at that point, because there didn't seem to be any way that this could actually be happening. But it was. Andy was tugging at my jumper and I had to turn round. *I had to turn round!*

When I faced him his face was full of doubt and concern and bewilderment.

"I'm sorry…" he began, and I knew in that

instant that I'd been mistaken. I'd got the whole thing wrong. This wasn't my dad. He looked amazingly like I'd remembered Dad looking, but this man's voice was nothing like the same, and thinking about it, he was much younger too. Andy was right. I'd been seeing things with my primary-school eyes. I'd made a total prat of myself and now I had to say something.

"I'm sorry … my mistake. I thought you were…"

And then something terrible happened. I'd thought I was safe from the horror of my epilepsy. I thought my tablets had sorted it out, but I could feel that I was about to have an absence any second. It was the stress of the situation. Oh, who cared what it was. This was the day from hell. I wanted to rewind and start it again. I said a quick prayer that it would only last a few seconds and that neither Andy nor this poor stranger would be any the wiser, then I just managed to turn and face the shop window before my senses kind of evaporated.

"Tash! Tash! Are you all right?"

Andy's arm was round me and she was holding me as tightly as she could for such a small girl. The man was looking even more concerned and unsure of himself. I felt very touched, yet horribly worried.

"I'm OK," I muttered.

"Oh Tash, I thought you were going to faint. You didn't seem to be able to hear me."

"Come on, my dear. Come inside and sit down for a moment. Mrs Lambton will take care of you. You've obviously had a terrible shock. Don't worry about a thing."

They were guiding me inside. Andy's next words proved that she'd already finished my sentence and explained to the man that I'd thought he was my long-lost dad. "She hasn't seen him for over two years, you see."

"Oh, I'm so sorry."

"It's not your fault," I managed to utter, feeling a complete fool.

"Don't worry at all … but…"

I think he might have been about to ask me if that was me who had called after him the other day in the High Street. He changed his mind, though. He probably didn't want me to feel any more stupid. Mrs Lambton had appeared with a glass of water and had crouched down so she could look at my face. I really felt about as old as Peta at that moment.

"I'm OK, honestly," I said, wiping my hand quickly over my mouth to check I hadn't dribbled, because that's the very worst, most embarrassing thing about absences. Occasionally I'd dribbled in the past. My hand was dry, thank goodness. It looked as though I'd managed to get away with it because Andy said again, "I really thought you were going to faint, Tash. Are you sure you're all right now?"

"Yeah, I'm fine."

After more thank-yous and apologies on my part we left the estate agent's quickly before they could ask any further embarrassing questions, like why we weren't in school. Then we began to walk back in the direction we'd come.

"I'm really sorry about everything, Andy. You must think I'm a total div."

"Course I don't. Anyway, I've enjoyed having an adventure. It beats school any day."

"Talking of school, do you think we ought to go back there?"

"I suppose so," Andy agreed, then she looked down at herself. "Oh no, I haven't got my uniform on! I'll have to go home and change without Mum knowing."

"What about when you get home later? Won't she wonder how come you left in the morning without uniform and came back home wearing it?"

"Good thinking. I'll have to take these clothes in a bag to change into at the end of school."

So we went to school via Andy's. She was lucky because her mum was out, so she let herself in with the spare key and got changed, then we got to school just in time for lunch. We'd decided to say that we'd both had music exams that morning because we had the same teacher. There wouldn't be much of a problem as the register after lunch was so much more casual than the morning one.

It was Luce's turn to work after school, and as usual we all went down to the café. Luce kept on trying to get in on our conversation because she was afraid she was going to miss something interesting, but I assured her that I'd told all there was to tell when Andy and I had got back at lunchtime.

"Well, that gypsy was right, Tash, wasn't she?" said Leah. "I mean, a strange man *has* appeared unexpectedly in your life and he hasn't half caused a load of trouble!"

We all laughed about that, then I remembered what Andy had said about there being two fortune-tellers. I got her to tell the others her theory and they were all really excited about the thought that there might be a fortune-teller living somewhere nearby, who didn't look anything like a fortune-teller at all.

"Surely you'd recognize her if you saw her again, wouldn't you, Tash?"

"No, no chance. It was so smoky and dark in the tent, I could hardly see two centimetres away. Also, if there *were* two different women they were dressed identically. The dress was like an enormous billowing tent itself. It was impossible to see what the person underneath was like. And I told you that her face was covered with a yashmak, so the eyes were the only visible thing."

Fen adopted the tone of a television reporter and pretended she was addressing an imaginary camera.

"Well, we have precisely nothing to go on. So will detective Andy Sorrell solve the mystery and find the missing fortune-teller?" she said.

I glanced at Andy and saw that she was lost in thought. I had a private bet with myself that she would solve the mystery, because I knew Andy and she wouldn't let it go until she *had* done.

When I got home I heard Mum's voice talking to someone in the sitting room. I could also hear Peta's voice and one other little child's voice. I knew Danny probably wouldn't be home yet, and I was right. Peta was playing with Tom, and Mum was chatting with Ian, Tom's father. They were both drinking wine and seemed to be getting on with each other very well. Good. I liked Ian.

He asked me how my day at school had been. Because I didn't have anything interesting to report, and also because I was quite keen to get off the subject of this particular day, I decided impulsively to tell them both about Mrs Turner's visit yesterday. That was a good move because they were really interested and asked me loads of questions. Ian left not long afterwards, and almost as soon as he'd gone, Mum said, "I know, why don't I give Mrs Turner a ring and see if we can go and look at her birds and bees sometime?"

"Yes, that would be good!" I agreed enthusiastically, so Mum phoned straight away. Five minutes later, the visit was all arranged for the very next day! I couldn't believe it.

So on Saturday morning I woke up feeling happy that this was a new day and that I didn't have to worry about my dad any more. Mum suggested that I get Fen to come along, and then she said that she thought it might be nice if Peta had a friend, too. Apparently Mrs Turner had said that she didn't mind if there were six of us, not three. We knew Danny wouldn't be interested. It didn't take a genius to work out why Mum wanted Peta to have a friend. It was actually because *she*, Mum, wanted a friend. You can guess who came with us, can't you? Ian and Tom.

"So is Ian divorced too, Mum?" I asked outright, because I couldn't think of any subtle way of asking.

"No, his wife died eighteen months ago of multiple sclerosis," said Mum, looking quite upset for a moment.

"Oh, poor Ian," I said.

Mum nodded, then, thank goodness, Peta called out that she'd finished on the loo, so Mum had to go.

We picked Fen up on our way to Mrs Turner's, then met Ian and Tom when we got there. Everyone was so happy. No one could possibly have had any idea what a morning lay ahead of us.

Mrs Turner welcomed us like long-lost friends. She invited us into her house and gave the grown-ups coffee, Fen and me hot chocolate, and Peta and Tom milk. She naturally assumed that Ian was Mum's husband and my dad.

"Help yourself to sugar, Mr Johnston."

"Ian ... call me Ian, please."

"And I'm Helen," Mum added quickly but I could see a worried look flicking all over her face, because she knew she and Ian were still giving the impression that they were married.

"We're not actually married," she said, quite softly.

"Oh ... right," said Mrs Turner, who was obviously quite surprised but didn't want to show it.

"We're just good friends," added Ian.

"Oh ... right," repeated Mrs Turner, as though she didn't really want to know any more details. Typically, Tom and Peta filled her in anyway, in the way that only three-year-olds know how.

"My mummy's dead," Tom announced as he dipped his finger in a tiny bubble on the top of his milk, and said, "Pop!"

Poor Mrs Turner was looking very pale by now and I wasn't surprised. Fen and I gave each other a quick look, because we couldn't believe that Tom could say something so serious and sad so lightly. Ian must have caught our look.

"I'm afraid he's just too young to understand," he said, his face looking suddenly much older for a second, before Peta spoke.

"And I haven't got a daddy at all," she said, turning her palms up and spreading her fingers as if to show that she wasn't hiding one anywhere.

"I see," Mrs Turner said doubtfully, while getting up to put a few more biscuits on the plate.

Mum obviously thought that it was important to help poor Mrs Turner out at this point.

"Can't children be an embarrassment!" she said, with a little laugh that Ian joined in with.

"Especially these two," he added, rolling his eyes. "They really are two of the very worst of the species," he smiled, ruffling Tom's hair, and then the atmosphere improved considerably, thank goodness, but it didn't actually make Mrs Turner any the wiser about the situation.

A few minutes later we had a guided tour of Mrs Turner's garden, which was brilliant. It was one of those intricate gardens that was full of little patches of grass surrounded by lovely borders full of loads of different coloured flowers and plants and shrubs, then you only had to walk along a little path and there was another section that looked completely different. There were quite a few really tall shrubs, too, so that it felt more like lots of separate little gardens, rather than one great big one. Every so often we would come across a little bird-table, and we lifted Peta and Tom up so they could have a proper inspection. My arms got really tired with all that heaving Peta up. Either Fen was stronger or Tom was lighter, but Fen didn't seem at all tired.

Mum was in her element talking about all the different plants and shrubs, because she used to be a gardener. She worked at this huge great place and even rode one of those tractor lawnmower things.

Fen and I decided to get Peta and Tom involved in a game of hide and seek, so that Mum and Ian could have some peace. It was the most ridiculous game of hide and seek I've ever played. Peta wanted to hide first, so Fen and I turned our back with little Tom standing between us, then the three of us began to count to fifty. Tom got as far as four, then said every single number just after we'd said it, so the counting took for ever. I thought I ought to keep an eye on Peta, so when we'd got up to sixteen I turned round as discreetly as I could, to see where she was.

She had knelt down and curled up into a little ball with her hands over her face, right in the middle of the very nearest patch of lawn. She obviously thought that just because she couldn't see *us*, we wouldn't be able to see her. I nudged Fen over Tom's head and she turned to look at Peta. That set us off giggling because it was just so funny. But we didn't want either of the little ones to know we were laughing at them, so we just shook silently in between counting.

When we finally reached fifty the relief was enormous. "Come on, Tom, let's go and find Peta," we encouraged little Tom, who grinned up at us and nodded keenly, but stayed rooted to the spot. Fen took his hand and led him all over the place, saying, "Is she in here?" Then Tom looked up at Fen with big round eyes and said nothing, so I said, "No, she's not in here, is she? I wonder where she's hiding." Tom allowed himself to be led around by Fen and me for quite a few minutes like this. I don't think he had the faintest clue what we were doing, but he went along with it anyway, because it was obvious that Fen and I were having a good time. I glanced over at Peta several times, and the little curled-up ball never moved a muscle.

Eventually we thought the time had come to find Peta, so Fen took Tom to the little section of grass where Peta knelt patiently. At the moment that we were about to spot Peta, Fen put on a really dramatic tone and asked her usual, "*And is she here?"* Then we fully expected Tom to be hysterical with joy at having found Peta, but he simply stared at her for a moment then let go of Fen's hand, and knelt down in the same curled-up little ball right beside Peta. At this point Fen and I had to move away so we could crack up.

"Gen! Gen!" said Peta, rushing over to us.

"Gen! Gen!" said Tom, who was obviously not cut out to be leader of the pack.

"What's vis fing?" Peta then enquired, pointing to something behind us.

"Aha! You've spotted my pride and joy," Mrs Turner said, as the three adults came over to join us, and we all set eyes on the most spectacular piece of garden furniture. Fen and I recognized it as one of the things that Mrs Turner had talked to our PSE group about at school.

It was one of those amazingly cunning bird-houses, much bigger and more complicated than an ordinary bird-house. Mrs Turner showed us where there was birdseed hidden behind a tiny little door that you had to lift up. It would have been impossible for any bird to have the strength to lift the door, but the whole bird-house tested the intelligence of birds and proved that they *were* very clever.

To get the seed, a bird would have to sit on a little sort of ledge that was hidden right underneath a bird-bath, which was all part of the whole construction, and with its beak it would have to tap on the third little knob on a panel of knobs under the bird-bath. There were five knobs altogether and only one would work. When the bird tapped this knob it made a small round piece of wood come out of the wooden box above the bird-bath and slide down a piece of twine. At the end of the twine it touched a tiny spring which popped up and hit the catch which allowed the door to open. The bird had to realize that all this was going on and then go into the little box to get the seed. When it came out Mrs Turner would have to close the little door by hand.

"I'd seen this kind of thing on television," Mrs Turner explained to Mum and Ian, "and my husband said he'd try and make me one. It took him ages and ages but he really enjoyed the challenge. As soon as it was finished I put the seed inside and we sat on that little seat and waited and waited. Not many birds came at all. They all went to the other bird-tables, so I decided it wasn't a fair test at all. I mean, how could the poor birds know there was any food hidden behind that door?

"So what I did was to leave the door open for about a week, and by then lots of birds had got the idea that this was where their favourite food was. They didn't take much notice of the other bird-tables at all, and I always made sure there was food in here. Then one day I decided to shut the door and just see what happened. I sat on that little bench over there with a pair of binoculars. Sure enough, plenty of birds came round and they went straight to the door and pecked it and tapped it and tried to make it move, then flew round it again, then usually they gave up. Sometimes they'd only fly off a little way, then come back, as though they couldn't believe it was shut and they were just double-checking.

"One or two of the birds would examine the whole contraption. They'd fly round it, have a quick bath, and tap various other parts of it. But one sparrow went hopping up the twine and seemed a little more inquisitive than any other bird I'd seen up till then. The sparrow went underneath the bath and sat on the ledge and I began to get really excited. I knew it was just luck that it happened to be sitting there and it would be even luckier if it tapped the right knob with its beak, but incredibly it did. It actually tapped all the knobs. When the piece of wood goes down the twine, it makes a noise which attracts the bird's attention, so this little bird saw the whole process of the door opening. I bet it couldn't believe its luck. It went straight in there and helped itself to the seed, then flew away.

"As soon as it had gone I put more seed in there, then shut the door. I waited and waited but the sparrow never came back. Well, I say it never came back. It *may* have come back, because one sparrow looks very much like another, but I'd tried to take in as much detail as I could through the binoculars and I didn't think it came back.

"The next day I was out there again, sitting on the bench, and a sparrow flew straight to the door. I looked through the binoculars and I was pretty sure it was the same one that had tapped the knobs the day before. It hopped up the twine, jumped into the bird-bath, then flew on to the little ledge underneath. Then it flew off again and tried the door, but of course it wouldn't open, so it flew back to the ledge, and like a miracle it tapped the five knobs and flew back to the door. It knew precisely what would happen. It took the food and flew away."

"That's amazing!" breathed Mum.

"You're not kidding," agreed Ian. "And is that the only bird to crack the system?" he asked.

"I think so, yes," Mrs Turner replied. "But of course there might be other birds that can do it. I can't spend all my time out here watching what happens, much as I'd love to, but once or twice I've come out here to find the door open, and I've presumed that it's very likely to be the same bird doing it. I've seen him do it just three times altogether."

"Does it come every day?" I asked. "Might we

see it in action?"

"You might. It comes most days. But you know, it's even more intelligent than I thought, because the last time I was watching, it went straight to the ledge and tapped the third knob only. It must have worked out that this is the very knob to tap to set the thing in motion. And that's really clever, isn't it?"

"It certainly is," Mum agreed. "Let's wait for a while, can we?"

"Yes, of course. I want to show you my beehive, of course, and I think Tash was interested in the hedgerow, weren't you?"

"Yes, I'm interested in everything," I replied.

"That's what I like to hear," Mrs Turner smiled, and I thought, *Thank goodness I only said that in front of Fen. It sounded really goody-goody.*

Peta and Tom had been very quiet during the "intelligent bird" story. They'd sat down on the grass and removed their shoes and socks and T-shirts. They'd been making a little collection of tiny bits of grass, a daisy, a twig, a stone, a slug, a leaf and a rose petal. This little hoard was on top of their pile of clothes.

"It's amazing how easily contented you are when you're just three, isn't it?" Ian said, dragging his eyes from the bird-house and watching Tom and Peta with a smile on his face.

"What are you two playing?" Mum asked.

Peta jumped up, and realizing that she had everyone's attention, began to really play to the gallery by rushing round the little patch of lawn at a hundred miles an hour and shouting, "What are you two playing?" over and over again at the top of her voice.

After about ten seconds, Mum said, "Right, Peta, that's enough," and Peta burst into tears, which is most unlike her. It took us a moment to realize that something had happened to her, because she was sitting on the grass clutching her toe and beginning to scream, but the scream was a peculiar one. She didn't seem to be able to breathe properly.

For a few seconds everybody was mesmerized, then I saw the horror that came over Mrs Turner's face.

"She's been stung by a bee ... and she's obviously allergic. Bring her into the house as fast as you can. I'll get the antihistamine spray and phone the doctor. The ambulance won't be in time. Hurry!"

Chapter 6

It was Ian who scooped up Peta and ran after Mrs Turner into the house as the rest of us scurried fearfully behind. Mum was carrying Tom, her face white and set as we all listened to Peta's awful screams. By the time we were through the back door, Mrs Turner was spraying antihistamine on to Peta's red, swollen toe. Peta was sneezing and trying to speak, but couldn't get her breath. It could only have been a minute since she'd been stung, but her face was going blotchy as though she had nettle rash all over it. It was getting puffy, too. Mrs Turner was talking to the doctor.

"Peta, that's P-E-T-A Johnston… About a minute ago … antihistamine … yes, all the symptoms … yes, we'll be with you in ten minutes … yes … thank you … bye." She put the phone down. "Right, I'm running you straight over to my own GP."

Mum got in the back and Ian handed her Peta, whose body was all floppy by then. She'd been sick, but there was no time to clean her up properly.

"Go with your mum, Tash," Ian then said softly to me, as he opened the passenger door. "I'll drop Fen off on the way."

Mrs Turner was definitely exceeding the speed limit, but nobody said a word. I couldn't have spoken even if I'd wanted to, because there was a huge lump in my throat which was really hurting. Mum's face was a mask. She began to talk very rapidly and softly to Peta. I couldn't hear what she was saying because of the noise of the engine.

"Won't be long now," Mrs Turner said. "Less than five minutes." But though her words should have been comforting, her voice didn't match somehow. It sounded like she was having trouble speaking, too.

We came to a red traffic light. I began counting and with every second that passed the journey became more and more unbearable. What it must have been like for Mum I didn't know. She was bent over the still form of Peta. At one point when I turned round I caught a glimpse of Peta's skin, and felt my mouth go completely dry as I saw that it was tinged with a faint blue.

"Come on, come on, move," Mrs Turner said in a low, threatening whisper to the traffic light.

Only I could possibly have heard her. I thought if the traffic lights didn't change in a second I'd scream. They did, but the traffic in front of us seemed to take ages to get going. As soon as she could, Mrs Turner put her foot down and started darting in and out of the traffic, ignoring the horns of the cars around her and the angry looks of their drivers. She just drove on, tight-lipped, leaning forward, shoulders hunched. Then she screeched into the surgery drive and pulled up right in the middle of the car park.

It only took us half a minute to get into the surgery. The receptionist was waiting for us, businesslike but worried, as she held back the door for us to pass.

"Go on … straight in," she said softly.

The doctor was right there. He looked briefly at Peta and so did I. She was blue. I was holding back my tears even though the lump in my throat was agony, but I couldn't hold them any longer. They were squeezing their way out of my eyes and blurring my vision. When my vision cleared I saw the doctor putting the needle down on the table. He'd already given Peta an injection. He must have had it all ready before we'd even arrived.

Peta's eyes were rolling by now and she was starting to lose consciousness. Her face was totally puffy.

"Adrenalin," said the doctor, giving us only the briefest word of explanation.

All this time Mum had been holding Peta and saying nothing. The doctor guided her gently to a chair and patted her shoulder as he bent down to look carefully at Peta and take her pulse. He kept his fingers on her pulse and his eyes on her face.

"The adrenalin will immediately reverse the drop in blood pressure," he explained softly.

After less than a minute, Peta's colour began to come back, and the doctor gave a small sigh of relief, which I think only I noticed. "I'm going to give her an injection of piriton and hydrocortisone to get rid of the symptoms and set up the long-term repair."

When he said that, Mum at last took her eyes off Peta's face and whispered, "She *is* going to be all right, isn't she?"

As the doctor wiped over the injections, his fingers went straight back to Peta's wrist.

"Yes, her pulse is back," he answered after a moment.

Mum's eyes widened and a question formed on her lips. I knew what she was going to ask. It was, "You mean, Peta was dead?" But she didn't ask it. She closed her eyes for a second and bent her head over Peta's still floppy little body and kissed her puffy face very gently.

A minute later Peta's colour was back to normal

and the puffiness had begun to go down. She scratched her body briefly and snuggled into Mum. A nurse was hovering in the background and she asked us all if we'd like a cup of tea. I looked round, expecting to see Mrs Turner, but she'd stayed in the waiting room.

"We go home now," said a little weak voice as Mum stood up, and I don't know if it was the sound of Peta's voice or just the shock of everything, but Mum flopped straight back down into the chair. Her legs weren't strong enough to stand up. I took Peta gently off her so that she could get up slowly without any weight on her, and stretch her legs a bit.

"Yes, we'll be going home very very soon," I whispered back to my precious little sister.

"We've called for an ambulance because Peta needs to stay in hospital under observation tonight, Mrs Johnston. You'll be able to stay with her. And at the same time they'll test the rest of the family for bee-sting allergy. It's not very common, but as you now know it's extremely serious. It was the adrenalin that effectively saved Peta's life, so the hospital will arrange for you to have a special pack with all that is needed to inject her immediately if ever she should be stung again. The pack should be with her, probably strapped round her waist, wherever she goes."

The doctor had a very sympathetic voice and a

kind face, and he was explaining everything to Mum in just the way I knew she would have liked. It was very straight and to the point.

"So, it was actually Mrs Turner's prompt action that saved Peta's life," Mum said slowly.

"That's right," answered the doctor. "Another few minutes and it would have been too late."

The rest of the day felt like a dream. Mum went in the ambulance with Peta to the hospital. She had thanked Mrs Turner profusely and Mrs Turner had said how awfully guilty she felt that it had happened in *her* garden. We hadn't been anywhere near the bees at the time. It was all a massive coincidence. Mum assured Mrs Turner that it absolutely wasn't her fault at all, and that she would be forever grateful to her for saving Peta's life. It was lucky Mrs Turner was a beekeeper because it took a bee-keeper to recognize the symptoms of bee-sting allergy so quickly, and to know exactly what to do and how important it was to act fast.

Ian dropped Tom off at their next-door neighbour's, who was also the child minder, then he ran me home and I sorted out a change of clothing for Peta and an overnight bag for Mum. He waited outside for me and I was glad he did because Danny was in the house and I had to explain to him all that had happened. I started by telling him that Peta was completely all right and out of danger, then I told him everything. I don't think I'd ever held Danny's attention quite so well. He wanted to go to the hospital, but I could tell he didn't want to go in Ian's car. Well, I've already mentioned, haven't I, that Danny can't handle anything to do with Mum and other men. In the end I went out to Ian and said that my brother wanted to come too, and was that OK?

"Of course it's OK," Ian said, so I went back into the house and told Danny that Ian was waiting.

Danny looked really surly as he got into the front of the car, as though Ian didn't have any right to be involving himself with something that was so personal to our family. Ian could probably sense that Danny wasn't all that happy, and he tried to get him to relax by talking about the fantastic bird-table contraption, but unfortunately that only made matters worse because Danny simply hated the idea of Ian having a nice time with our family. Only the occasional grunt was forthcoming from Danny and I felt myself getting more and more embarrassed in the back. It was one big relief when we finally got to the hospital.

Both Danny and I were tested for bee-sting allergy at the hospital and it turned out that neither of us was allergic. Mum already knew she wasn't allergic herself, because she'd been stung twice before and had had no reaction.

"Thank goodness for that," she said with a smile when we heard the news. I think it was probably her first smile since the awful bee-sting moment.

Ian had only come into the hospital briefly to check that Peta and Mum were both all right. Danny had watched Ian and Mum's communication like a hawk, and he seemed to cheer up when it was perfectly obvious that Ian's concern was no more than that of a friend. I think it was Ian's casual parting words that really cheered Danny up, though.

"See you around then," he had said to Mum. "Hope Peta will be fully recovered soon. I'm sure she will." Then he had gone, and Mum hadn't seemed at all bothered until she'd realized that Danny and I were stuck at the hospital with no way of getting home.

"Don't worry, I'll sort something out," Danny told her confidently, and once we'd been tested, he phoned Kim, who got her mum to come and get us. Leah came along for the ride, so I had someone else to tell the whole story to then. Just before we actually set off, though, I saw Ian's car draw up nearby. Danny's mouth set in a firm line.

"What's he doing back again so soon?" he snarled.

"Shan't be a sec, Pat," I said as I quickly got out of the car. Ian spotted me immediately.

"Oh Tash, there you are. I suddenly realized how thoughtless I'd been driving off and leaving you and Danny stuck here, so I came straight back."

I was about to thank him very much for his trouble, and explain that we'd got a lift, when Danny appeared at my side and said, "We've made our own arrangements, thank you."

Ian looked taken aback but only for a second. I glared at Danny, as Ian said, "Oh, all right, as long as you're OK."

"Ian's just come specially back, actually, Danny," I said pointedly.

"No, it was no trouble at all. Anyway, if you're sorted out I'll be going."

He gave me a really nice smile but just nodded at Danny. I was glad. Danny didn't deserve more than a nod. He was being so hateful.

"What do you have to be so rude for?" I hissed at him as we went back to Pat's car.

"You wouldn't understand," he replied gruffly.

"Try me," I said, but then we had to stop the conversation because we were at the car.

Pat dropped Leah and me at the café where I knew Fen would be on duty. Jaimini and Luce were there, and immediately beckoned us to go and join them. Fen came out of the kitchen, spotted me and rushed over. She obviously hadn't been out of the kitchen since she'd got there, otherwise she would have told the others all about Peta.

"How is she? How is she? Have you been tested too? Are you positive?"

"She's fine, and I'm negative," I answered, while Luce looked from one to the other of us and said, "What? What? Who? Who's fine? What do you mean, positive?"

Just then, Andy came in and we beckoned her over.

"How is she? Is she OK? It must have been awful, Tash. Leah phoned me when Danny had phoned Kim," Andy said quickly, as she sat down.

At this point Luce had had more than she could bear. In desperation, she lifted the tiniest corner of her mouth and spoke in a barely under-standable voice, "What are you all on about? Tell me, before I burst."

So for the third time that day I went through the whole story, as Fen got back to work. There were plenty of gasps and pale faces as the tale unfolded, and it didn't surprise me, because right in the middle of telling the story for this third time it suddenly really hit me how close we had come to losing Peta.

Long after I'd finished talking and we'd moved on to other things, one or other of them kept coming back and asking me another little detail, until Fen suddenly came out of the kitchen and said, "Come in here, Tash. Look at this."

She was being very mysterious, and Luce wanted to come too, but as Fen pointed out, Jan wouldn't like it if too many people were hanging about in the kitchen. I couldn't work out what it was she was going to show me, and even when I saw it, I couldn't understand what all the fuss was about.

"There!" she said, her finger pointing to a tablecloth that she'd been ironing.

"What?"

"See that mark?"

I peered at the tablecloth and saw a green stain. "Yes, what is it?"

Kevin turned round at that point and said it was green jelly from another planet that had mysteriously dropped on to the tablecloth in the middle of the night.

"Oh, be quiet, Kev!" Fen told him off for joking when she was trying to be serious.

"Well, it's certainly green," I said, "but what is it?"

"Don't you see?" Fen asked patiently, as though she'd made a very obvious connection between a leaky pipe and a pool of water, but I was too thick to work it out.

"No, I don't see. Can't you just *tell* me?" I said finally, beginning to get exasperated.

"It's nail varnish," she answered, with a knowing gleam in her eye.

Even then I didn't click on. "Nail varnish? Green? Are you sure?"

"Yes."

"Um … so what?"

"Tash, think! Green nail varnish. Who have you seen wearing green nail varnish lately?"

I thought, and of course it came to me instantly. "Gypsy Tirrasana!"

"Exactly."

"So…" My poor brain was still struggling to make the connection that Fen found so easy.

"So, that means that she's been *in* here, *in* this café, *at* one of these tables."

"What? Doing her nails?" Kevin asked in an afraid-you-must-have-got-that-wrong tone of voice. "You don't sit in a café doing your nails with green nail varnish, do you?"

"Why not?" Fen came back at him quickly.

"Because Jan wouldn't allow it for one thing."

"Wouldn't allow what?" asked Jan, swinging through the door at that very moment.

"Wouldn't allow anyone to paint their nails at a table in there," Kevin answered, nodding at the door, to show what he meant by "in there".

"How did you find out about that?" asked Jan. "*I* certainly didn't tell you."

"Tell us what?"

"Tell you about how I had to speak to that dreadful woman about the awful smell of her nail varnish remover, not to mention the revolting green nail varnish and the fact that she was getting it all over the tablecloth."

"What awful woman?" asked Fen.

"That big woman with the scarf and the repulsive pink and purple velour trouser suit. I tried to persuade her to go to the loo to do it but she wouldn't."

"Was it glittery nail varnish?" I asked, peering at the tablecloth to see if any little trace of glitter remained.

"It was so glittery it dazzled me," Jan said, shaking her head at me as though I was mad to ask such a question. I suppose it must have seemed rather a strange detail to want to know.

"That's her," I said to Fen. "Let's go and tell Andy."

"It doesn't take two of you to tell Andy," Jan said, putting her hand out to stop Fen from rushing away. "You're on duty, Fenella Brooks. Let's see a bit of work going on round here, if you please."

Fen sighed and I slipped back to our table and told Andy what we'd discovered.

"And has she been back in here since the fair went?" she asked.

"I didn't ask that," I admitted, feeling rather silly.

We checked with Jan, who said that the woman had only been in three times ever, and those three times were when the fair was in Cableden, so that proved that *she* was the gypsy and that she must have moved on when the fair went.

"But that still doesn't necessarily prove that there were two different fortune-tellers," said Jaimini, getting into the mystery.

"I think it does," I said slowly and thoughtfully, as a piece of jigsaw puzzle slotted into place in my mind. "Hang on a sec. I'm just going to ask Jan something."

"Jan, I know you'll think I'm mad," I said a moment later, approaching Jan in the kitchen, "but that woman painting her nails, were the nails long or short?"

Jan gave me a half-smile as though this *must* be a joke and at any minute I would crack up. Then when she realized that I was perfectly serious she frowned and looked down. "Long," she said, sounding very definite.

"Could they have been false nails, do you think?"

"No."

Again she sounded totally sure of herself, but I wanted to know how she *could* be so sure.

"How do you know?" I asked, tentatively. I didn't want her to get sick of me asking questions.

"Because she happened to say to me that she

108

wished she'd splashed out on a pair of pre-painted false ones, because it was so much less trouble, as the polish didn't chip so easily on those."

"Thanks, Jan," I said, giving her a big smile and getting out of her way quickly before I got on her nerves.

"There *are* two of them," I told the others.

"How come?" Andy asked.

"Because the first fortune-teller had short, neat nails which weren't varnished at all. They were really clean. I remember distinctly. Jan's just told me that the woman who was in here definitely had long nails and they *weren't* false. Apparently the woman made some comment to Jan about how much easier it would be if she'd simply bought false, pre-painted nails."

"Brilliant! Now we've got something to go on," Andy said, in her go-for-it voice.

"What? Clean nails?" asked Luce. "Yeah, that certainly narrows it down a bit, doesn't it?" she went on, sarcastically.

"It's not just clean nails, Luce. It's a whole lot more than that. For a start, we now know which is the fortune-teller to believe, don't we?"

Chapter 7

That evening as soon as I got the chance to talk to Danny, I grabbed it. He nearly always goes out on Saturday evenings, or occasionally stays in with Kim, but on this Saturday he must have decided to stay in on his own. You see how difficult it is sussing Danny out. In most ways he's kind and nice, it's just his problem with Mum and her relationships that changes his character. I wasn't looking forward to talking to him, but on the other hand I couldn't bear the thought of always having his moods to put up with whenever any adult male appeared in our house.

"Danny, can we talk?" I began, as I flopped down in a chair next to the settee where Danny was sprawled out watching television.

"As long as the name 'Ian' doesn't enter the conversation," he replied without even looking up.

"OK, it's a deal."

"Go on, then. Fire away."

"Well, can you switch the telly off?"

He used the control to turn the volume down, but still didn't honour me by looking at me. He was irritating me already, but I knew I mustn't be riled so easily or the conversation would degenerate into a row in no time at all.

"You've got to face the fact that Mum is a woman, and however much you don't like it, she has every right to be happy."

I thought that was a very good start. I'd prepared that sentence carefully and I was quite pleased with the way it sounded. I eyed Danny to see how he was taking this first round of bullets. His face showed nothing, so I decided to carry on.

"You've also got to face the fact that not every single man who ever appears in her life is necessarily a potential boyfriend..."

That bit was prepared too, and I'd only got one more sentence to go, but Danny's reaction to my wise and wonderful speech was still nil.

"I don't see every man who appears in her life as a potential boyfriend," he came back at me. Good. This was better. He was defending himself.

"You might not realize you're doing it, but you do, Danny," I said as gently as I could.

"No, I don't. When did I last do that then?"

"Well, this afternoon with Ian…"

The moment the name was off my lips I realized I'd walked straight into his cleverly-laid trap.

"You said you wouldn't mention that guy and you've mentioned him already," Danny shot at me, then he grabbed the controls and switched the volume on the television up higher than he'd had it before. Suddenly I snapped.

"God, you make me sick!"

He didn't react at all, which made me even sicker. Right, I'd show him. I'd bring a bit of worry into his smug little life. I marched out of the room and out of the house before I could change my mind. Once outside, I walked and walked, all the time going over and over the conversation but changing the lines so that Danny was made to look a fool and I came out on top, and he promised to change his attitude in future. It gave me great satisfaction playing all these imaginary conversations in my head, but after about ten minutes of marching along in a temper I realized that I was getting cold and it was getting dark.

And Danny must be getting worried, I thought with satisfaction. Good. Then I began to feel anxious that Mum might phone from the hospital and Danny would say that I'd gone out and he didn't know where I was, and then poor Mum would worry. The last thing I wanted was to give Mum any more cause for worry. I stopped walking and stood still and thought hard.

The best plan I could think of was to phone Mum at the hospital and say that I was on my way to Fen's. Then I really would go to Fen's, but I wouldn't tell Danny. I'd just leave him to stew. I'd tell Fen, though, and then if the phone rang Fen could quickly answer it, but I'd instruct her to say, "No, sorry, Danny, I haven't seen Tash all evening." That would be good. That would make him suffer. That would make him think twice about refusing to communicate with me in the future. There was a phone box just at the top of the road I was walking along.

Inside the phone box, my hands explored my jeans pockets and my jacket pockets and there was no ten-pence piece. Sugar! I'd just have to go to Fen's and phone the hospital from there.

I half walked and half ran to Fen's, because it was getting darker by the minute. When I got there the house looked ominously empty and a little stirring of unease crept into my bones. I rang the bell and waited and waited, but I knew it was pointless. There was no one in. I couldn't work it out. Fen hadn't said anything about a family outing or anything. It was most unusual for them all to be out. Fen has two little sisters, one aged nine and one aged five.

My feet dragged as I set off back home. I was going to look really stupid creeping back in when I'd stormed out. Maybe Danny hadn't even noticed that I'd gone. Or maybe he *had* noticed but he didn't actually care. I'd probably get back there to find Kim and Danny eating fish and chips and watching some gripping video. They'd probably take one look at me and their hearts would sink because they'd realize they hadn't got the house to themselves after all. That pesty sister *had* to come back, didn't she?

The more I thought along these lines, the more bitter I felt. How I wished I had a ten-pence piece so I could phone Danny and tell him a thing or two. Then, like a flash it came to me. I didn't need a ten-pence piece to phone home, did I? I could reverse the charges. What if Danny didn't accept the reversed charges? No, he wouldn't be that callous, would he? I hurried back to the phone box.

On the way I passed a man who was obviously drunk. He was lurching about terribly. If it had been day time I would probably have just crossed the road and carried on walking without worrying too much, but there's something about the dark that makes your whole view of things change. My heart beat faster and I instantly thought *danger*. What if he was carrying a weapon? I gave him a very wide berth as I passed him, but he didn't seem even to be aware of me, so I then gave myself a firm talking to about being pathetic. All the same, I turned round after I'd passed him, just to check he hadn't stopped or anything. He hadn't.

In the phone box I dialled one hundred and asked the operator for a reverse charges call and told her the number. She asked for my name, then I heard her putting me through and asking Danny if he'd accept the charges for a call from Tash Johnston. The next moment I was through.

"Where the hell are you?" Danny began.

Good. He was really worried, *and* mad.

"What's it to you?"

I knew I was being ridiculous, but I couldn't help myself. The very sound of his voice brought back the frustration I'd felt when he'd refused to discuss his big problem.

"Don't be stupid, Tash. Just come back home, OK?"

He was sounding more like the real Danny now, and I could tell he was worried about me being out on my own in the dark. It was nice to have that little bit of power over him.

"I've no intention of coming home unless you promise you'll talk to me about your stupid big hang-up."

"Where are you phoning from?"

"I'm not telling you."

"Oh, act your age not your shoe size, for goodness' sake."

"What, like you, you mean?"

"Cut it out, Tash."

I knew I was sounding really childish but I couldn't stop. I wanted Danny to be sorry and to beg me to come home and to talk to me properly.

"This conversation is really boring, you know. Just come home straight away and we'll talk."

This was better. Now we were getting somewhere. I was about to push the bargain a little further when a sharp tapping noise made me jump. I gasped as I realized that the drunk man I'd just passed was standing right outside the phone box, tapping on the glass with a coin, and leering in at me with his face pressed against the glass.

"What's the matter?" asked Danny, urgently. The gasp must have come over as terrified.

"There's a man. He's right outside the phone box. Oh Danny, he looks awful – really scary. What should I do?" I was almost in tears I felt so frightened.

"Tell me where you are, quick."

"I'm at the bottom of Denton Street."

"Stay there. Pretend you're still talking on the phone. I'll be there in five minutes."

With that the line went dead and there was only my heartbeat and the awful tapping every few seconds to keep me company. I didn't dare look at the man. I just kept moving my lips, pretending to talk, and praying that Danny would be quicker than five minutes, but I knew there was no way he could be any quicker than five minutes, even if he ran hard all the way.

I knew Danny told me to stay put in the phone box, but what if the man got really mad, because he was in a hurry to use the phone? Maybe I ought to rush out quickly and run away. I was on the point of doing this when a car drew up right outside the phone box. This would be a good moment to rush out, while other people were close by. The man wouldn't dare chase me or anything with someone watching. I knew I had to act immediately so I put the phone down before I could change my mind, yanked open the door to the phone box and went full pelt straight into Ian!

"Hey, steady on, what's the matter...? Tash?" He had seen the man by then. "Come on, get into the car with me." He walked with me round to the passenger seat and opened the door for me to get in before getting back into the driver's seat himself.

"He's had too much to drink. I should think he's completely harmless, but just looks pretty awful. What are you doing out here on your own anyway?"

There was no way I could say I'd been arguing

with Danny and stormed out of the house in a temper. I tried to invent something which sounded better, but finished up saying, "It's a long story … but thanks for rescuing me. I was petrified when that guy started tapping on the window like that."

"I'm not surprised. Were you on your way somewhere, or shall I run you home?"

At that point I remembered Danny. "No, it's OK, I'll walk." I could just imagine how angry Danny would be if he turned up to find me sitting having a cosy chat with Ian in his car.

"I wouldn't dream of letting you walk, Tash. It's far too dark."

"No, honestly, Danny's coming to meet me, actually. He'll be here any minute now."

I looked round and saw that the drunk man had disappeared, but there was a figure in the distance running towards us. It *had* to be Danny, and I *had* to get out of this car, quickly.

"There he is now. Thanks again for rescuing me, Ian. Bye." And with that I leapt out of the car and started walking very quickly towards Danny. By now I could clearly see that it *was* Danny. I kept up a prayer that there would be no sign of Ian's car by the time Danny got right up to me, or at least that it would be impossible to tell that it was Ian in the dark. Why wasn't he driving off? I knew the answer to that. It was because he wanted to check it really *was* Danny, and that I was safe, before he drove away.

"Are you OK? Where's the man gone?" puffed Danny as he approached me. He looked so full of concern at that moment that I wondered how I'd ever argued with him.

"The man went staggering off, thank goodness. Thank's for coming out, Danny. I really was petrified."

"You sounded it. Come on."

Then, just when I thought there was definitely no danger of him noticing Ian, Danny's eyes swivelled to the car.

"Hang on a sec … isn't that … it *is*, isn't it? It's that Ian bloke! What's he doing here? And don't try and tell me it's a coincidence."

The nasty, scowly, unreasonable Danny was back. "Look, Danny," I said in a pleading voice, "Ian just happened to show up to use the phone, I swear, and then I came rushing out obviously scared out of my wits and he told me to get into his car."

"Oh great, so I needn't have bothered giving myself a coronary rushing to the rescue then, because the great Ian got here first. You phoned *him*, Tash, didn't you? Tell me the truth, for goodness' sake."

"No, I didn't. I promise. You can go and ask him if you want. He's still sitting there."

"No thanks, I wouldn't talk to him if you paid me."

At that point Ian drove off, waving as he went by. I gave him a very overenthusiastic wave to make up for Danny's bad manners.

"You know what your problem is, Danny, you're jealous."

"Course I'm not. Don't be stupid. Why should I be jealous of someone as old as him? And what's there to be jealous about anyway? You're not my girlfriend or anything."

I didn't bother to answer. This was a dead-end conversation. I just wanted to get home and go to bed; then the morning would come sooner and Mum and Peta would be back home and everything would be back to normal – well, as normal as we'd ever get. I made a resolution there and then to wait a little while until Mum had nothing on her mind, then I'd ask her to have a go at Danny herself, and make him realize that he had got to stop being jealous all the time.

When we got home I was quite surprised to find Kim there. She jumped up, looking wide-eyed and worried, and immediately asked me if I was OK. She'd obviously been there when I'd phoned, and Danny had left her to come and get me. No wonder he wasn't all that pleased. It still wasn't an excuse for flying off the handle about Ian, though.

I went up to my room and phoned Fen's house to see if anyone was there. Fen answered the phone.

"Hi, Fen, I thought you weren't in. It's me."

"Hi, you. Well, I *am* in."

"I came round earlier and the house was in darkness."

"Oh, we went out for a Chinese. Dad's treat."

"I'm on my own with Danny and Kim. As you can imagine, it's great."

"Do you want me to come over?"

"Yeah, could you? That would be really good."

So Fen stayed the night and we spent all evening in my room listening to music and talking.

"I've been thinking, Tash…"

"Mm…"

"We've got to track that fortune-teller down. After all, she's been right about everything, hasn't she?"

I frowned. So many dramatic things had been happening, I hadn't given the fortune-teller a thought.

"Peta's been in great danger…"

"Yes, you're right," I said, staring straight ahead of me and concentrating. "Then there were the lines of traffic. She said she could see lines of traffic in the way. Omigod! That's incredible, Fen! What else did I tell you that she said?"

"The little cat in danger…"

"Oh no, I've still got that to come."

"And I hate to say this, Tash, but the man you thought was your dad obviously wasn't the man she meant at all. I very subtly got Mum to talk about the estate agent's next to Meads. The guy you spoke to has worked there for years. Mum was positively waxing lyrical about what a nice guy he is. Apparently, she used to play badminton with him, or something."

"So who is the man that the fortune-teller mentions then?"

"Maybe it's Ian?" Fen said, cautiously.

"No. It couldn't be."

"Why not?"

"Because he doesn't fit the description."

"What is the description?"

"Well, for a start she said something about water ... yes, she said that he probably came from across water. Well, Ian didn't."

"Do you know that?"

"Well, not exactly, but he lives here in Cableden, doesn't he?"

"How long has he lived here for?"

"I think mum said about eighteen months ... no ... it was eighteen months ago when his wife died. It's probably only about a year then."

"You don't actually know, do you?"

"No, but he didn't come across water to get here, I'm sure."

"But, Tash, you can't say that. You *don't* know it for sure."

"Well, what about this then? He's definitely not trouble. I mean, he's not getting me into hot water, or whatever she said."

"What exactly *did* she say?"

"That he would bring trouble…"

"And *that's* certainly right."

"And that he *is* trouble, and that's definitely not right, because he's a really nice guy."

"But look at the facts, Tash. The fortune-teller has got everything else right… Mrs Turner was the woman who was pleased with you at school, Peta's been in awful danger and the lines of traffic made the danger even greater, and this guy Ian is causing a load of trouble in your life right now."

"What about the little cat?"

"Maybe that's still to come."

"What about the tall blond boyfriend? I haven't exactly noticed too many tall blond boys lining up to take me out, have you?" I asked sarcastically, because I wanted to lighten the mood. It was getting me scared, all this talk of little animals in danger and men who were trouble.

"Who said the tall blond boy was a boyfriend?"

"The gypsy, the second time I went."

"But she's a fake, remember? What did the first one say?"

"She said something about a tall blond boy who

was older than me, who was going to be very significant."

"So, no mention of boyfriends?"

"No, I suppose not."

"That must be Danny, then. He's been pretty significant this evening, hasn't he?"

At that point I gave in. I'd known Fen was right all along, I just hadn't wanted to admit it because it was too scary. I nodded miserably.

"But what can I do about it all, Fen? There's nothing I can do, is there, because it's all going to come true anyway."

She frowned and thought hard before replying.

"I reckon you need to find out from your mum where Ian used to live, and if it was in France or somewhere, then you need to tell Danny everything that the fortune-teller said, and between the two of you, you need to keep your mum away from Ian, which probably also means keeping Peta away from Tom."

That night it took me ages to get to sleep, and when I did finally sleep I dreamt about Ian leaping over puddles which turned into ponds which turned into lakes. And all the time he'd got a really nasty expression on his face, and he was after us. But Danny was one step ahead of him, bustling Mum and Peta and me into helicopters and trains and boats, anything to try and escape Ian.

It was a restless, awful night.

Chapter 8

The following morning, about an hour after Fen had gone, Mum and Peta came home.

"I hope you've bofe been lookin after Scribble and Boo Boo baby while I've been in ve hospital, you two," were Peta's first words as she came through the door. Danny and I both laughed and I picked her up to give her a big cuddle, but she wriggled down again and went looking round the house for Scribble.

"What a transformation!" I said to Mum.

"I know. It's unbelievable, isn't it?" said Mum, with a tired smile. "I keep counting my blessings. We were so close to losing her, you know."

I gave Mum a big hug and Danny made us all tea. It was so lovely to have them both back. Mum told us that she hadn't been able to sleep much in the hospital because it was so hot. Apparently Peta had been pretty well back to normal after only a couple of hours, and it had been quite a task keeping her entertained during the afternoon.

"So what did you do, Mum?" I asked her.

"Well, Peta was desperate to visit some people, as she put it, so in the end, I took her to one of the women's wards and to the delight of all the patients, she went from bed to bed chatting away about her bee-sting and the bird-table thing. It was quite interesting that she didn't seem to have any recollection of anything that happened after Ian picked her up. She thought it was Ian who picked her up and put her in the ambulance, because she couldn't remember a thing about going to the doctor's, or even being at the doctor's."

I glanced over at Danny when the dreaded name came up, and even though he had his back to me at the time, I could practically feel him bristling.

"Ian was brilliant, wasn't he?" I said, rather cruelly, I suppose.

"Yes, he was. I must thank him," Mum said.

"Anyone would have done the same, wouldn't they?" Danny put in.

Mum looked slightly taken aback, but just said, "Well … yes, I suppose so." And Danny then gave me a look as if to say, "See?"

"Has Ian lived in Cableden long?" I asked, as

casually as I could, because I thought I ought to try and get my questions in here and now while we were actually talking about him.

"No, he's only been here about a month, I think."

"Where did he used to live before?"

I had asked the six million dollar question and I could feel my heart banging against my ribs, as I waited for the reply.

"The Isle of Wight."

My insides seemed to dislodge for a moment.

"The Isle of Wight?" I repeated quietly, still vainly hoping that I might have misheard.

"Yes. I was surprised too. I could imagine it the other way round, but I couldn't work out what should attract someone from the Isle of Wight to a place like Cableden. Still, there's no accounting for taste, is there?"

"So what *did* attract him?" asked Danny, trying hard not to scowl.

"I'm not sure. I must ask him one of these days. Anyway, I'm starving. Who wants some pizza?"

I tried to sound enthusiastic, but I very much doubted if I'd be able to swallow anything for a while. I went upstairs and phoned Fen.

"He came from the Isle of Wight about a month ago," I announced the moment Fen came on the line.

She gasped, then was silent. I could imagine

her on the other end with a frown on her face, her brain racing away.

"Right, you know what we said. You've got to tell Danny."

"Yes, you're right."

"Tell him all the details. Make sure you get it across how serious this is."

When I'd rung off I went straight to Danny's room because I'd heard him go in there when I'd been talking to Fen. As soon as I announced that I had something really serious to tell him, Danny put his head in his hands as if he completely despaired of me. I just ignored that gesture and got on with telling him in as a few words as possible what the fortune-teller had said, and exactly what had happened, including the bit about the tall blond boy.

Danny didn't interrupt at all while I was talking, and I really thought I was getting through to him, but when I'd finished he said, "If you honestly believe that anything that's happened is any more than complete coincidence, you need your head examining." Then he got up and went out of his room. I suddenly felt completely drained. Danny was impossible. I got a piece of paper out of his drawer and wrote the following:

Danny,

I couldn't care less about anything else, I only want to make sure that Mum doesn't come to any harm. If you can't even see why I'm worried after all that's happened, then you're the one who needs his head examining. T.

Danny and I said as little as possible to each other for the rest of the day and it was quite a relief when he went out. I wanted to go out too, but I didn't dare leave Mum on her own in case she got in touch with Ian. This is ridiculous, I thought; I can't stay at Mum's side for ever. I'm going to have to take some kind of action.

The next day at school, the moment the bell went for morning break the six of us went down to the netball courts and Fen and I filled everybody in on all our discussions. Jaimini had some paper with her, and between us we composed the following advert to go in the local paper.

I am trying to trace the fortune-teller who was at the fair in Cableden last Monday evening. This is important. Please write to Tanya Roberts at The Café, High Street, Cableden.

We had decided that it was best to change my name and use The Café for the address. I didn't want Mum or anybody I knew finding out about this. I was going to warn Jan that if any mail came for Tanya Roberts, it was for me because Tanya Roberts was my pen-name for this competition I'd entered.

"Now all you can do is keep an eye on Scribble

and Boo and, of course, your mum," Fen summarized.

"Hmm," said Andy.

"What's that 'hmm' for?" asked Leah

"I think you can do more than that. I think you ought to find out much more about Ian. Encourage you mum to invite him over and really quiz him about things. You'd soon find out if he has anything to hide, or if there is anything dodgy about him."

"I don't think I would, actually. I think I'm biased. I like him too much."

"Well, I'd be able to," Andy said. "I know, why don't you tell your mum that I'm going to bring Sebastien over to see Peta, and suggest that Tom comes too?"

"That's a good idea."

I could hardly wait to get home so I could put the suggestion to Mum, but as it happened, I didn't need to bother. After school we all went down to the café. Jaimini was on duty so she went round to the back, but the rest of us went in by the main door, and guess who were the first people I saw? Mum and Ian with Peta and Tom!

"It's *him*!" I hissed at the others, then they got us a table and I went straight over to Mum and Ian.

"Hello, Tasha," said Peta, "I done vis," and she thrust a big splodgy painting under my nose. I was about to ask what it was, when Tom giggled and thrust his own little masterpiece under my nose, with the single word, "Vis!" I admired them both, but realized after no time at all that they'd moved on to something else. In this case it was tearing up the napkins into little shreds, and letting them fall down on to the table like a shower of rain while they sang, "Pitter patter rain drops," over and over again.

Ian and Mum smiled at their children, then at each other.

"What are you lot all doing here?" I asked Mum, trying not to sound accusing.

"Ian and I found we were collecting Tom and Peta at exactly the same moment from the nursery school, so we decided we'd pop in here for a quick coffee. I only just said – didn't I, Ian – that I bet you lot would appear at any moment!"

Mum sounded very relaxed. She called out hello to the others, then Ian offered to treat us all to a cake. Not one of us accepted, because I think we all felt that it seemed somehow wrong to be accepting cakes from someone you suspected as being up to no good.

"Don't tell me you're all on diets," Ian called over, with a grin for the others.

They laughed nervously, and I babbled on about how we weren't all that hungry, then I suddenly clicked on to what Mum had just said.

"Peta doesn't normally go to nursery school on Mondays."

"No, I know, but I'm behind with my work at home and I really needed peace and quiet for phone calls and letters and things."

"What do *you* do, Ian?" I asked, pulling up a chair and sitting down as casually as I could. Mum smiled at Ian and me. I think she was thinking how maturely I was acting all of a sudden.

"I work from home, too," he replied, with a sort of hesitant look at Mum.

"You may as well know that Ian and I are thinking of joining forces," Mum said, lowering her voice. "It's very early days yet, but my holiday business is expanding all the time, and I really can't manage it on my own any more. Ian's in the process of negotiating with Jim Sadler to buy the building, then we've got all sorts of plans for the future of the business."

"Oh, right," I said, and I couldn't think of anything to add to that, so I called out to Andy before I had time to change my mind. She came over with a friendly smile on her face.

"This is Ian, this is Andy," I introduced them.

"Funnily enough, Andy and I were only just arranging for Andy's little brother, Sebastien, to come over and play with Peta next time Andy has to babysit him, and we wondered if Tom wanted to come too."

"Well, that's a very kind offer, girls. I'm certainly not going to turn down an offer like that in a hurry!"

"Now shall we go to your house, Ian?" piped up Peta.

I looked at Mum to see if this was already arranged.

"First we're going home to get Scribble to take him to the vet's, aren't we?" Mum reminded Peta. "Then I only said we'd go to Ian's if there's any time left, all right?"

Peta nodded and let another handful of paper-napkin rain flutter down. Jan appeared behind her at that moment and tickled her under her arms.

"This looks a good place to tickle," she said with a laugh as Peta giggled like mad and called Jan a "very naughty tickle person".

"Right! We'd better be going," Mum said, looking at her watch. "Do you want to come, Tash?"

I decided I would, so I said bye to the others. Andy, who'd been totally silent for the last few minutes, said she'd phone me later about the English homework. I knew that she actually meant that she'd phone me to tell me what she thought about Ian.

When we got home and were about to set off again with Scribble safely in the travel basket, Mum looked at the calendar and said, "Oh no! I thought the appointment was for a quarter to five, but it's a quarter to six. What a shame we rushed away from the café."

"Take Boo Boo for a walk?" asked Peta, sounding at her most sensible.

"Yes, that's a good idea," Mum beamed at Peta. "Let's go to the forest."

As Scribble was curled up perfectly happily in the cat basket, we decided to take him with us and go straight on to the vet's from the forest, so Boo went into the back of the car and off we went.

The forest is the best place for miles to take dogs for a walk, because there are so many little places to explore. Boo wagged his tail in ecstasy when he jumped out of the car.

"Scribble must be the only cat in the whole world who doesn't mind car journeys," Mum commented, when we saw that Scribble was still curled up fast asleep in the basket. "He'll be all right there. We'll only be gone for twenty minutes."

"And the car will be locked, won't it?"

"Yes, of course."

So off we went. It was a lovely day and it seemed like the sun was a huge beacon winking at us in morse code through the tall, thin pine trees. Boo went rushing off, then came careering back as though he was running some crazy sort of race. Peta laughed and shouted and kicked leaves, and

Mum and I looked at each other and thought for the hundredth time how lucky we were to have Peta with us.

"We'd better be making tracks," said Mum, calling to Boo, who came trotting obediently to her side. In the car, Scribble slept peacefully on, though he did open one eye to see who had interrupted his lovely snooze.

"Come on, Boo, in you get," said Mum, heaving Boo on to his rug in the hatchback, but the naughty thing jumped straight out again and ran away.

"Boo!" called Mum, but it was as though he had scented something and he was running further and further away to find it.

"Oh, no! He's going miles away," I said.

"Ve silly ole doggy," commented Peta, striking her forehead with the palm of her hand in a very adult gesture, which looked so funny on a three-year-old.

Mum and I took turns to yell at the tops of our voices to Boo, but there was no sign of him anywhere.

"We're going to be late for the vet's at this rate," Mum said, looking worried.

"The vet will understand, won't he?" I said.

"I ought to at least phone, though."

"Why don't *you* go to the vet's and I'll stay here and look for Boo," I offered.

"I don't want to leave you here on your own, Tash."

"I'll be OK."

"I wouldn't be happy about leaving you, I'm sorry. It won't be long till it'll be dark."

"But we can't leave Boo here."

We stayed another ten minutes, shouting all the time for Boo, but there was no sign of him and Mum insisted that she wasn't letting me stay there on my own.

"We'll come back after the vet's."

"But it'll be dark after the vet's."

In the end Mum decided that we'd just have to forget the vet's and apologize the following day. She drove the car very slowly through the main drag of the forest as far as she could, even though it wasn't really allowed, and we had the windows rolled down and kept calling out to Boo. Finally when Peta was whining on and on, and Scribble was making pitiful mewing noises, and it was getting very cold and rather dark, Mum said we'd have to give up and come back the next day.

"Couldn't we notify the police?"

"They're unlikely to do anything until he's been missing a bit longer," Mum replied.

So, home we went, and on the way I went cold all over as I realized that here was just one more thing which had come true. Right, Danny would *have* to believe me now. But what about Mum and her big business venture with Ian? She'd sounded so excited about it, I couldn't get in the way of that, could I?

What a mess. What a complete *mess*. And the paper wouldn't be out till Friday, and then it would probably take a couple of days for a letter to get to me. And meanwhile little Boo was all on his own in the forest.

At half-past eight in the evening I could bear it no longer. I begged Mum to just drive with me to the forest.

"Just to the entrance, Mum, *please*."

"Do you mind babysitting Peta, Danny?" she asked finally.

"No, course not." Danny had been really shaken by what had happened to Boo, I could tell. I'd caught him staring into space several times with a worried look on his face. I was pretty sure that at long last he was beginning to think that maybe I didn't need my head examining after all.

All the way to the forest I said a prayer, *Please let Boo be there, please let Boo be there*, over and over again. As soon as we drew up I opened my door and Mum said, "It's too dark to go looking now, you know." I was about to argue that I'd got a torch and we could just go a little way, when a small, wet animal jumped on to my lap and began to lick my face as though I was the tastiest ice cream in the whole world.

"Boo! Where have you been?" I asked, clasping him tight with one hand while closing the door quickly with the other.

"You naughty boy, Boo," said Mum, but she couldn't make her voice sound cross however hard she tried.

I looked an absolute wreck by the time we got home, but I didn't care. Danny's face broke into a big smile of relief when he saw who we'd brought back with us, and Boo got more attention that evening than I think he'd ever had before. He wasn't injured in any way, he was just extremely dirty. Bathing him was certainly an interesting exercise! Danny and I did that together. It was the first companionable thing we'd done together for ages. When we'd more or less finished Danny suddenly said, "I've been thinking about what you said, and I think you're right. I'm going to keep an eye on Ian for the next few days. Don't say anything to anyone about this, but I won't be going to school much."

"Are you going to tell Kim?" I immediately asked, because then I could really find out how serious this was in Danny's eyes. I knew he told Kim just about everything.

"Nope," he said. "Not for the moment."

Andy rang shortly after that and I told her what had happened to Boo.

"I thought it was supposed to be a cat in

danger?" she quizzed me.

I thought for a while. "It was the second fortune-teller who said about the cat. The first one said it was a small animal," I said slowly, as I thought back to Monday and Tuesday evenings.

"You really must sort out in your mind who said what, Tash. It's important. You can ignore everything the second woman said. Just concentrate on the first one. Are you sure you've remembered correctly about the man?"

I racked my brain, but everything was just spinning round. "I think so," I said finally.

"Keep thinking," was Andy's advice.

"What did you think of Ian anyway?" I asked.

"I think he's really nice," she replied.

"But he can't be underneath, can he?"

"Why not?"

"Because everything else that the fortune-teller said has come true. Absolutely everything! I'd love to think that Ian is a perfectly harmless guy, but I can't risk thinking like that," I told her quite emotionally.

"There's no way that Ian is trouble. I'm majorly certain about that," Andy insisted.

"You mean you're still not totally convinced that the fortune-teller has any talent? You think it's all coincidence?"

"No, I don't. I think she's got a load of talent, but I don't think Ian is the man."

"What! Well, you don't think it's the guy I thought was Dad, do you?"

"No."

"So you think I've still got the pleasure of meeting the strange man who brings trouble and comes across water, do you?"

"I don't know, Tash. I really don't know. All I feel sure about is that there's nothing wrong with Ian."

After that we rang off quite quickly because I was never going to be able to agree with Andy. I decided to phone Fen and tell her the latest.

"Guess what happened to Boo?" I began dramatically.

"Oh, no! What?"

So I told her the "forest" story. When I'd finished I told her Danny's reaction, and also what Andy had said.

"I agree with Danny," she told me softly. "I'm glad he's taking it all seriously. What do you think he's going to do about Ian, though?"

"Just kind of spy on him, I suppose."

"At least you're not on your own any more, Tash."

We rang off a couple of minutes later and I went down to watch television with Mum for a bit.

"Just think, the night before last I was cooped up in that hot, hot hospital," Mum said. "I can't tell you how lovely it is to be home."

"I wonder if Peta has any idea how dangerous her bee-sting was?" I asked Mum.

"I don't think she does," Mum smiled. "In fact, one of the ladies in the ward that we visited asked her what she was in hospital for and Peta said, "I don't know. What are *you* here for?"

"And what was the lady's answer?"

"Pneumonia. She sounded very raspy, but she was pleased to see us. Apparently she doesn't have any relatives round here and she tends to keep herself to herself, so we were her only visitors."

"Poor thing. It must be horrible not to have any visitors when you're in hospital."

"Mm. She *did* say something rather interesting about that."

"What?"

"She said she had the feeling she was going to have some visitors quite soon. It crossed my mind that she was going a bit doolally or something, but I tried to look interested and said, 'Really?' and she tapped the cards that were on her bedside cabinet and said, 'Well, it's in the cards, you know.' Then she gave me a very searching look. It quite unnerved me. I took Peta to the next bed as soon as I politely could."

"She tapped the cards? What did she do that for?"

"Well, they were tarot cards... You know, for

141

seeing into the future. She obviously fancied herself as a fortune-teller!"

Mum jumped up to make a cup of coffee and I sat frozen to the settee, my brain in a spin. There couldn't be that many fortune-tellers in Cableden. This lady must be the one I'd seen at the fair. She must be. I *had* to go and see her. As I had that thought I took a sharp intake of breath, because that's exactly what she'd said to Mum. She was expecting some visitors. This was incredible. Double incredible. I'd phone Fen.

"You look as though you're in a trance," Mum said, coming back with her coffee and sitting down.

"No, I'm just day-dreaming," I answered, very casually. "That woman in the hospital, did she look like a fortune-teller? You know, big gold earrings and lots of black curly hair?"

"No, not at all. I think that's partly why I was so taken aback. She had short brown hair and a very sweet face. Just her eyes were rather piercing, but she didn't wear any jewellery. She looked completely plain in fact."

"Oh, that *is* unusual," I said, as lightly as I could while my insides churned away. "I bet she had long glittery nails though, didn't she?"

"Not even that, no. As far as I can remember her nails were very short and clean."

Chapter 9

"What are you doing today then, Mum?" asked Danny, at the breakfast table. It sounded so unusual to hear Danny talking like this to Mum that I immediately realized what he was up to. I glanced at Mum, and she looked pleasantly surprised that Danny was taking an interest.

"I'm working here this morning, then I'm taking Peta to the nursery school so I can have a meeting with Ian. Did Tash tell you about our new venture?"

"No," he replied, rather too sharply, throwing an irritated look in my direction.

So Mum explained to Danny how she and Ian were hoping to go into business together, and Danny asked her if she thought it was a good idea going into business with someone she'd only known for such a short time. Mum replied that she wasn't going to rush into anything without good, sound financial advice, and added that the venture was very much in its early stages.

"Who's the financial adviser then?" asked Danny.

"I've not decided yet," answered Mum, then she looked carefully at Danny. "There's nothing to worry about, you know, Danny. I trust Ian completely."

"That's what I'm worried about," Danny came back quickly. "You can't afford to trust someone when you've only just met them."

"Look, Danny," said Mum, putting down the plates she was about to take to the sink. "I'm not planning on having a relationship with Ian, if that's what you're worried about. I'm simply trying to get the very best out of my holiday business, and there's no way I can carry on on my own. Then fate lands me Ian out of the blue. His qualifications and experience are perfect and he's really interested in joining me. So we're simply trying to work out if that's viable. There's nothing wrong with that."

That was quite a speech for Mum and I could tell that she was just beginning to feel irritated by Danny being overprotective. Danny didn't say any more, just ate his breakfast quickly and went out to get ready. I wondered what he was planning to do and when we crossed on the stairs

I asked him in a whisper.

"I've already done it," he replied, also in a whisper.

"What?"

"Punctured one of Mum's tyres. It'll be completely flat by the time she wants to take Peta to nursery school."

I clapped my hand to my mouth and swallowed hard. Mum was going to be hopping mad, but I had to hand it to Danny: that was quite a clever plan of his. I'd already told Danny about the woman Mum had met in hospital, though I hadn't mentioned my plan to go and see her myself. I'd found out what ward she was in and I'd phoned Fen. Fen and I were going to go to school, then sneak out at morning break. We thought we'd be back by lunchtime, so there wouldn't be any need to make any excuses.

Before assembly, we told Leah, Jaimini and Luce all the latest dramatic news, then at morning break, we slipped out through the gap in the hedge. We'd both got a jumper to put on in place of the black school one, so we just needed to take our ties off and we didn't look as though we were in uniform at all. It would be easy to change back afterwards as well.

We had to catch a bus to get to the hospital and we both got very nervous in the bus queue. It seemed such a very public place to be and we were dreading seeing anyone we knew. By some miracle a bus came after only five minutes and there wasn't a single person we knew in sight. It took twenty minutes to get to the hospital and the relief when we got there without being seen by anyone who mattered, was enormous.

We found our way to the right ward and had a quick look through the double doors before going in. Imagine my horror when I set eyes on Mum, Peta, Ian and Tom, at one of the beds!

"What's your mum doing here?" asked Fen, as shocked as I was.

"I haven't the faintest idea. Be careful, she might see us. She's facing this way." Peta and Tom were each sitting on one of Ian's knees. They were blocking my view of the person in the bed, but Ian suddenly got up and reached over for some cards which were on the bedside cabinet. As he moved I caught sight of the patient. It was definitely the woman who had told my fortune at the fair.

She was wearing a nightdress instead of the flamboyant gypsy dress. Her hair was short and straight, not a single black ringlet in sight, but I still knew that this was the same woman. Her eyes were grey and piercing, her hands with the neat short nails were folded on the bed clothes. Mum was talking and smiling and nodding.

"Can you catch what she's saying, Tash?" Fen asked.

"Not really. I heard what she said just then, though. 'Flat'. Flat what? Flat tyre. She's telling the woman about her flat tyre. That's how come Ian had to bring her."

"But what's she doing here in the first place?" asked Fen.

"Mum's a soft touch. I expect she felt sorry for the poor lady and decided to give her a bit of company as she doesn't get any visitors."

It was impossible to hear anything else that Mum was saying and Fen and I were getting restless. "What are we going to do?" asked Fen. "We can't hang about here. Your mum might see us."

"What are you two doing here?" came a voice from behind us, which made us both go rigid. I spun round.

"Danny! What are *you* doing here?"

"I'm trying to follow Mum and … him. It's not easy, I can tell you. I found out where he lived from Mum, then went round there. Practically as soon as I arrived he came out of the front door with his kid and started to strap him into the car. The neighbour called out that it was a lovely morning for going out for a drive – nosy woman – and he replied that he was helping out a friend with a flat tyre who wanted to visit someone in hospital. I put two and two together and came straight here. I've been all over this hospital looking for them. How did you know they were here?"

"I didn't. We came so that I could talk to that fortune-teller Mum mentioned. We got the shock of our lives to find Mum and Ian here, too."

"So what do we do now?" asked Fen.

"Omigod! I don't think we've got much choice now."

Peta had seen me. You didn't have to have superhuman hearing to know that she'd called out, "There's Tash!" as she pointed gleefully at the window in the door. I ducked instinctively and we were about to beat a hasty retreat so that Mum would assume that Peta had been mistaken, when a nurse swung through the double doors leaving the three of us completely open to view.

"Tash! Danny!" said Mum, jumping to her feet in alarm. Then she came out of the ward and confronted us. She looked worried at first.

"What on earth are you doing here? Why aren't you at school?"

Danny and I looked at each other. It was a *shall we?* look.

"It's impossible to explain quickly, Mum," Danny began, while Mum looked at him, her worried eyes beginning to fill with mistrust. Danny glanced behind her to where Ian was still sitting by the woman's bed, minding his own business.

"You see, Tash had her fortune told by someone," he said, lowering his voice and speaking rapidly. "And everything has come true. She was told that a little animal was in danger, but would be all right in the end. She was told that a little girl was in great danger and there were lines and lines of traffic…"

Mum's mouth dropped open. "Go on," she said quietly. Danny had really got her attention now. The mistrusting look had gone. In its place was alarm.

"She was told that a woman was going to be really pleased with her at school. That turned out to be that bee-keeper woman… She was told that a tall blond boy was going to be playing a big part in her life and that's me."

"And what part is that, Danny, may I ask? Troublemaker?"

Mum's expression of alarm had been slowly turning sour, and now she was looking quite angry. There were two spots of colour in her cheeks. I couldn't work it out. After all, Danny hadn't even got to the Ian bit yet.

"And I expect she was told that her mother mustn't get involved with any men called Ian, was she?" snapped Mum in a cold voice. "I suppose that's why I found my papers all disturbed this morning, is it?" Mum gave Danny the toughest look I think I've ever seen her give him. "You've been going through my private papers, Danny, and that is *not on*!"

"I was only trying to find out where he lived... That's a detail anyway," Danny came back at her, his voice raised.

"And what about the flat tyre? Is that a detail too?"

"I only did it to try and protect you, you know," Danny said aggressively, and that's when Ian appeared with Peta and Tom at his side.

"Can I help?" he asked Mum, with a look of concern in his eyes.

The sight of Ian being so helpful made Danny snap. "No, you can't. *You're* the problem. Why can't you leave Mum alone?" he rounded on Ian, eyes glinting.

Mum was in a terrible temper too. Her eyes were flashing and her voice was low and cold. "This time you've overstepped the mark, Danny. I've tried to take your feelings into consideration, but you're acting like an idiot."

"No, *you're* the idiot, Mum, for not seeing the danger, even when we spell it out to you. Tell her, Tash."

Danny looked at me with desperate eyes, but I didn't know what to say. It had all been said.

"D-Danny's only thinking of you, Mum. It's just that all the rest has come true."

"Why don't you go and ask the fortune-teller?"

Fen was hissing in my ear.

"Can I offer anyone a lift?" asked Ian, sounding and looking as though he was barely hanging on to his temper.

"Yes, thank you, Ian," Mum said in a quiet, controlled voice. "I can't apologize enough for my son's behaviour. If you could possibly take the three of them back to school and me back home I'd be more than grateful."

"Forget it," said Danny, "and don't say I didn't warn you, Mum." With that he went striding off down the corridor.

Mum closed her eyes and held her breath, as though this might somehow magically make all her problems disappear, then she opened them again and shook her head slowly.

"Go and see Mrs Carr if you must, Tash," she said in a flat voice. "I'll be in the cafeteria on the ground floor. Don't be long."

So Fen and I went into the ward and approached the fortune-teller, while Mum, Ian, Peta and Tom went off in the opposite direction. Danny had clearly damaged Mum's friendship with Ian, because it was obvious Ian was not happy and he didn't seem to be the kind of man who would stand around being abused like that.

"Hello, my dears. Are you coming to see me? I *am* the lucky one today."

"Mrs Carr, do you remember me?" I asked.

"No. Should I?" she answered with a bright smile.

"You told my fortune at the fair last Monday evening."

"Ah, yes. I was only there because Gypsy Tirrasana was in one of her famous sulks, you know."

"But do you remember me?"

"Yes, I think I do," she said, thoughtfully.

"You told me that there would be a man appearing in my life, a stranger, who would come from across water ... do you remember?"

"Not really ... but what did you want to know? I don't always get it right, you know..."

She sounded like a slightly batty, rather sweet old lady. I had been really searching her eyes and I was sure that this was the same lady I had spoken to at the fair. She *must* be, because she'd actually said she was there, but here in the hospital she seemed so different. The stirrings of unease were creeping round me, making me shiver. Had I made a terrible mistake? Was it just that mystical atmosphere in the gypsy's tent that had convinced me that she was genuine?

"You got everything else right, but I'm ... worried about the man because I don't know who it is, and you said he'd bring trouble."

"Did I say he'd come from across water?" She was looking puzzled.

"Yes … I think so."

Her eyes were beginning to focus on me. The dotty look had completely gone. She took my palms and turned them over and looked at them carefully.

"I remember these hands."

"So can you tell me about the man?" I said, feeling excited that we were getting somewhere. Fen was leaning forwards and I was willing Mrs Carr to help us out here.

"You must understand, my dear, that fortune-telling is a hit and miss thing. There are a lot of believers and a lot of non-believers in the world. I'm a believer. There are also a lot of gifted people and a lot of fakes. I'm lucky. I've been blessed with a gift. I've often got things right, but I've sometimes got things wrong. I don't make things up – ever. But if I could see the whole future mapped out like a book, I'd be making *my* fortune instead of reading other people's. The only way I can describe what I have is by saying it's like flashes of vision. I don't like doing it at the fair, but every year they come to Cableden, and because they know about me, they get me to come and sit in for Madam Tantrum with the long green nails. I should never have set foot out of my house last Monday. Look where it's got me."

"But can you tell me about the man, or can't you do it without your crystal ball?"

She laughed when I said that. "That's just a gimmick. Well, not entirely. It helps you to focus."

Then she turned thoughtful again. "I'm not well enough to get the feeling of being tuned in, I'm afraid…"

"Is there nothing you can tell me?" I said, in an almost pleading voice.

"I'm trying to remember how I felt about this man the last time…" She was staring into my eyes again. "I remember the water coming into it … but I don't think I said he was coming across water… Certainly water … but I think the water was more important… I'm not sure. The feeling really isn't there, dear, I'm afraid. This hospital atmosphere doesn't help, but then again maybe the danger's over."

I sighed and thanked her anyway, then got up to go.

"Ask about Ian?" hissed Fen, so I sat down again.

"You know that man who was with Mum just now?"

"Oh, was that your mum?" Her face lit up.

"Yes. Um … you don't think the man is anything, um, dangerous, do you."

"No, I think he's a sweetie, and I'm only sorry I'm not twenty years younger!" She spluttered at her own wit. Immediately, I regretted having asked her that question, because she'd switched back to her dotty old lady mode and I didn't know what to believe now.

Fen and I discussed it on our way down to the hospital cafeteria.

"That hasn't really helped much, has it?" Fen commented, sounding as disappointed as I felt.

"I wish I'd never gone to the stupid fair in the first place," I said, sulkily. "I think I'm just going to forget it all and get on with my life, which is what Andy and Jaimini told me to do in the first place."

"What about Danny?"

"I don't know," I said with a sigh. I'd forgotten about Danny.

"And what about Ian?"

"I bet Mum'll make Danny apologize. Only Danny'll probably refuse."

We'd reached the cafeteria by then. I braced myself as Fen and I approached Mum and Ian's table. I was slightly surprised that Ian was still there. He'd looked so tight-lipped and hacked off that I thought he might have just disappeared and left Mum to her own devices. Mum was looking tense. Ian was looking uncomfortable. They both jumped up in a very businesslike manner when they saw Fen and me.

"Ready?" Mum asked, without asking me any questions at all about what Mrs Carr may have said. I thought this was rather odd, but I decided it was best to keep quiet, the atmosphere round here was so bad. Peta and Tom were prattling on quite happily, and it was a relief to have their chatter and noise to fill up the awkward silence that lasted all the way back to the car.

Mum and Ian strapped the little ones in the back, then Fen and I squashed in beside them while Mum and Ian got in the front. We set off in silence and after no time at all Peta and Tom both fell asleep, which meant that we didn't even have their childish noise to keep the temperature above freezing point. This really was the journey from hell. No, it wasn't. I'd already had the journey from hell on Saturday morning with poor little Peta. When we arrived at school, Fen and I got out, and Mum said, "See you after school, Tash," in quite a cold voice.

"Yeah, see you. Thanks for the lift, Ian," I mumbled.

"That's all right," he managed to answer, but I thought that would probably be the last I'd see of Ian. I couldn't imagine their business project going ahead after all that had happened.

"What a mess," I said to Fen. "Ian's really cross, isn't he?"

"Yes, he is."

We changed back into our school uniform as soon as the car was out of sight, and as I was changing I was trying to puzzle something out.

"If he really *was* trouble, he wouldn't be cross, would he? He'd still be trying to give the impression that everything was fine so that he could stay in touch with Mum."

"Or maybe he *was* trouble, but now the trouble's over," Fen said thoughtfully. "Let's see what Andy thinks."

As we ate lunch in the canteen, we told the others about the hospital visit.

"What a mess," breathed Luce, as though a mess was a really cool thing to be in.

"I'll try and pump Kim to find out what Danny's told her," Leah said.

"What do you think, Jaimes?" asked Luce. "Come on, you're the brainy one."

"I think you need to pretend you never went to the fair, and just try to act normally," was Jaimini's answer. "After all, whatever's going to happen, is going to happen. Not that I think anything *will* happen, of course."

"What do *you* think, Andy?"

"I think there's still a piece of the puzzle missing," Andy replied. "But I'm certain that Ian is nothing to do with anything. I feel really sorry for that guy."

"I wonder what your mum's thinking right now," Luce said, staring ahead of her.

"I don't know. At first she was furious, but

when we got down to the café, I think she was fed up. She looked so relieved when we appeared."

"Maybe she and Ian had had a big row or something."

"Well, Ian *did* look cross, it's true."

After school, the others went down to the café. I was going to go straight home, but at the last minute I couldn't face it.

"I'll just come for a few minutes then," I told the others.

Leah was on duty and the place was pretty busy. Jan brought our drinks, then went to serve the table next to us. I wasn't really listening to her, but something she said made me pay attention. She was chatting to two women who were regulars at the café.

"I know… It's awful, isn't it? He wasn't all that old, you know. Such a sad end, isn't it?"

Where had I heard those words before? *A sad end.* I racked my brains, and it came flooding back. That's what Mrs Carr had said to me last Monday in that tent. *A stranger … I see trouble for you. He is trouble. And water … something about water. Trouble and deep water. Such a sad end.*

One of the women that Jan was talking to was showing the newspaper to Jan. The headline was "Drunk man drowns in reservoir". The picture was of a man whom I recognized. An electric shock ran through my body. This was the man who had scared me in the phone box.

I stood up to go.

"Where are you going, Tash? You've not finished your drink."

"I think I've just found the missing piece of the jigsaw puzzle," I replied.

Chapter 10

When I left the café so mysteriously like that, the others gulped back their drinks and followed me.

"What's the missing piece then?" Luce asked me, eyes wide.

"Tell us what's going on, Tash," begged Leah.

"D'you need any help?" asked Fen.

"Don't do anything rash," advised Jaimini.

"Leave her alone," said Andy.

"I'll tell you later," I called, because they'd hung back on Andy's advice. I ran most of the way home, desperate to start repairing things, and praying that it wasn't too late.

The scene that met me in the sitting room made me think that my prayer couldn't have been answered. Peta was nowhere to be seen, Boo was curled up in a corner, Scribble was curled up beside him, and Mum and Danny were going at each other hammer and tongs.

"I don't need you interfering in my life like this, Danny! Why couldn't you just tell me your fears instead of taking the law into your own hands? You've ruined my business plans."

"Because you don't listen! You refuse to believe that anyone else's opinion might possibly count. You think your opinion is the only one that's ever right."

"That's unfair. I've always listened to you. It's pure selfishness that makes you act as you do…"

At that point they saw me and Mum broke off mid-sentence, closed her eyes briefly, sighed deeply, then flopped down in a chair.

"I give up. I really do."

"It's not Ian, Danny!" I said.

"What do you mean?" Danny asked warily.

"Look!" I picked up the regional newspaper from the coffee table. The article and picture were on the front page. I showed it to Danny.

"That's him. That's the man who scared me when I was in the phone box. He's drowned. *He* was the stranger, not Ian. Jan was talking about it in the café, and she suddenly said something which jogged my memory. '*Such a sad end.*' The moment I heard those words I remembered the fortune-teller saying the very same thing, then her other words came back. She said she saw trouble for me, then she said that he *was* trouble and that there was something about water … trouble and getting in deep water. I thought she meant that *I* would be getting in deep water. I didn't realize she meant *him*. And I didn't realize she was talking literally either. I thought it was just an expression she was using…"

"So where did all this about the stranger coming from across water come from?" asked Danny, beginning to look embarrassed.

"It's my fault. It's all my fault," I confessed. "You see, I went back on the Tuesday night to see the fortune-teller again, and it was all smoky in the tent and she was wearing exactly the same clothes and earrings and everything, and at that time I naturally assumed it was the same person, but it turned out that it wasn't. The second one was the gypsy from the fair who can't tell fortunes properly. As soon as I'd worked that out, with the help of Andy, I tried to remember exactly what I'd been told on Monday and what I'd been told on Tuesday. I thought I'd remembered everything, and I'd decided to ignore all the Tuesday stuff, but the one thing I still got confused about was who said what about the water. Now I remember. Mrs Carr never ever mentioned anything about someone coming from across water. That was Gypsy Tirrasana…"

"Hold on, hold on," said Mum, leaning forward. "Why didn't you tell me any of this before, Tash?"

"Because I didn't think you'd believe me. I thought you'd just think I was trying to get you away from Ian, and I didn't want to worry you after all that you'd been through with Peta ... and anyway Danny thought it was a load of rubbish..."

Mum looked at Danny. He went a bit pink and started shuffling about self-consciously. "I only thought that at first, then when more and more things started happening, I changed my mind."

"So why did you automatically assume that the stranger that Mrs Carr was talking about was Ian?" asked Mum.

I nearly told her that I'd thought it was Dad at first, but I decided that that would just complicate matters.

"He was the only man who had recently appeared in my life. Then when you told me he'd come from the Isle of Wight, I felt really scared. I thought this *must* be the stranger she meant, and that he was going to harm you or something. So I told Danny. Surely you can see why we were worried, Mum ... I mean, after all that happened to Peta and to Boo?"

"Yes ... yes, I can see," she said softly, as she leant back again and gave us both a sad sort of smile. "I *can* see, but I just wish ... anyway, it doesn't matter. It's too late now."

"What do you mean?" I asked fearfully.

"Well, Ian's obviously furious but he's just far too

polite to make a big scene about it. He must think I've totally cocked up bringing up my family."

Danny and I looked at Mum and I could tell Danny felt the same as me, if the expression on his face was anything to go by.

"You've not cocked up, Mum," he said quietly.

"I'm sorry. I've wrecked everything, haven't I?"

"No, it's my fault," I said. "I'm the one who wound you all up."

"One thing's for sure: it's *not* Ian's fault. What am I going to do about that?"

Danny shrugged, then suddenly left the room and left the house. Mum sighed yet again and I thought I ought to try and say something positive for a change.

"Do you know who's been right about Ian all the way through this, even when nobody else agreed with her?"

"Who?"

"Andy. Come to think of it, she's been right about everything. She didn't believe in Gypsy Tirrasana. She worked out that there must have been two different fortune-tellers. She realized that Mrs Carr wasn't a fake, though. She met Ian for two minutes and said that he was a really nice guy and there was no way he was trouble. Then, finally, to cap it all, she said that she thought there was a piece of the jigsaw puzzle missing. And she was right, because as soon as Jan started talking about that man who had come to a sad end, the missing piece fell into place."

"She sounds like one clever girl," Mum said, with that same half-smile. Poor Mum, I thought, looking at her leaning back into the chair like that. She must feel absolutely drained. She was obviously sad to lose Ian as a friend as well as a business contact.

"I wonder what Danny's doing," I ventured.

"I dread to think," she replied, wearily.

"Where's Peta?" I then tried, thinking this was safer ground to be on.

"She's playing with Alice Munroe," answered Mum, then she picked up the paper and started reading it, so I went upstairs to do my homework.

The phone rang about twenty minutes later and Mum answered it. Almost immediately she called to me to come down.

"That was Ian," she said with a frown on her face.

"What did he say?" I asked in trepidation.

"He asked if I'd like to go round and have a drink with him."

"Really?" I was as puzzled as Mum.

"And he said to bring you and Peta."

"Oh!" This sounded too good to be true. It *was* too good to be true. "We can't go because of your flat tyre."

Mum's hopeful expression turned to one of

disappointment, so I quickly went outside to check that a miracle fairy mechanic hadn't popped round to mend it while we weren't looking. You can imagine how shocked I was to find that it *had* been mended. Well, not exactly mended, but a new tyre had been put on in its place. I hadn't even noticed when I'd come back from the café.

"Mum, there's a new tyre on!" I announced, crashing back into the house.

She rushed out to look, and after staring at it in disbelief for at least twenty seconds, she lifted up the hatchback, pulled back the carpet and told me that the old tyre was in there. Someone had put the spare tyre on the car.

"It must have been Danny," I said slowly, as I tried to work out when he could have done it.

"Anyway, let's go," said Mum. I didn't need telling twice.

We picked up Peta on the way and turned up on Ian's doorstep a few minutes later.

"Come in," he smiled.

Why was he smiling? Mum was being very cautious and hesitant, I noticed, and so was I. Only Peta went crashing in talking loudly about Alice Munroe's great big Lego "what is even bigger than the whole world!"

When we walked into the sitting room, there was Danny lying on the floor on his stomach, surrounded by cars and transporters and all sorts of brightly coloured toys, totally engrossed in fixing a wheel on to one of them, while Tom watched from very close quarters. With their heads bent close together like that, I noticed that their hair colour was identical. I don't know what Mum was noticing about the scene, but I've never seen her face soften so quickly before. She'd been so tense, and it was as though the cares of the world had been lifted from her shoulders in that one second. She smiled at Ian but he wasn't looking, so she smiled at me and I smiled back.

"Oh, hi," said Danny, looking up and noticing us, then he was straight back to his car mending.

"Getting a bit more practice at wheel-changing, are you, Danny?" asked Mum, with a wink at me.

Danny didn't look up or reply or anything, but I saw that he was grinning at the car he was fixing.

"We've been chatting," said Ian, handing Mum a glass of wine.

"Good?" asked Mum.

"Yes, very good," replied Ian.

"Good," said Mum, then they both burst out laughing at the ridiculousness of their conversation.

"I understand now," Ian went on.

"Good," Mum said again, but she didn't laugh

this time.

"Danny's agreed to babysit Tom and Peta together on Saturday, so you and I can go out to that Indian that's just opened in Raddlestone ... if you'd like...?"

"That would be nice."

This was like some kind of miracle. I don't know what Danny and Ian had been saying to each other, but somehow along the way the impossible seemed to have happened, because Danny had not only accepted Ian, he'd even agreed to babysit. Wonders would never cease! Ian must have made it quite plain to Danny that the friendship with Mum was just that – a friendship, and not a relationship. Well, who cared what they'd been saying? At long last peace had returned and that was all that mattered to me.

"What was the name of that friend of yours who was in the café the other day?" Ian suddenly asked me.

"Andy."

"Andy, that's right. I've been trying to think of her name. I knew it was a boy's name, but it's been really getting on my nerves that I couldn't remember what it was."

"Tash's just been telling me," Mum began hesitantly, "that Andy has been sticking up for you through thick and thin. Apparently she thought you were really nice."

"Really?" said Ian, looking very pleased. "Well, I must thank her sometime… Come to think of it, why not now?"

The rest of us all looked up blankly when he said that.

"Now?"

Ten minutes later we were heading for the café. Jan had been on the point of closing when Mum had phoned her from Ian's, but she said that she wasn't in a hurry and she'd love a bit more business because it had been rather quiet all afternoon. I'd phoned Fen and she'd set the chain in motion by phoning Andy.

When we arrived at the café, Leah and Kim were already there. I noticed Kim went straight up to Danny and asked him if he was OK. Then they were talking quietly for ages. One by one the others arrived and Jan put three tables together so we could all fit round them. I'd already told Fen briefly on the phone what the missing piece of jigsaw puzzle had been, and all about what had happened since. She had passed it on to Andy, who had passed it along the chain.

Ian sat next to Andy and thanked her for her "moral support" as he put it, then told her jokingly that she must be a great judge of character. We all laughed and then Luce asked me a bit too loudly whether Mum and Ian were going out together.

"No," I replied firmly, just in case Danny was

listening. But he wasn't. He and Kim were entertaining Peta and Tom by singing "The wheels on the bus go round and round". It was so funny listening to Danny singing a little kid's song in his deep voice. Kim thought it was hysterical. She couldn't sing for giggling.

A few minutes later I managed to talk to Danny on his own.

"What made you change the tyre, Dan?"

"I dunno. I was beginning to feel guilty, I suppose. I got a bus from the hospital straight away and when I got home and saw the car, I just decided that I'd try and do *something* right for a change. So I changed the tyre.

"What made me crossest of all, though, was that I was trying not to like Ian because I didn't want Mum getting involved with anyone. I couldn't help liking him, but I didn't want to. Then when you told me all that fortune-teller stuff, it got me thinking. I've never believed in that kind of thing, but in the end I suddenly realized that here was the perfect excuse for me to pin something on Ian. I just convinced myself that Mum would be in trouble or danger if she stayed with Ian, then I went about trying to get them apart."

Danny looked embarrassed again. It had taken a lot for him to tell me all that. I wanted to make him feel better.

"Whatever you said to Ian, it worked like a dream," I said.

"I just apologized, and we got talking. The more he talked, the more I realized that he was a really genuine sort of guy, and after all, his wife only died eighteen months ago. I found myself feeling really guilty for ever suspecting that he might be interested in Mum…"

"Anyway, Ian's probably a bit young for Mum," I added.

"Yes, and he explained to me that it was only the business that had brought them together. The more he talked, the better I felt."

"Thank goodness it's all sorted out," I said, but Danny didn't answer because Kim was calling him over. I watched him stroll over to her and thought what a good job it was that he wasn't watching Mum at that moment, because he would have flipped if he'd seen the expression in her eyes as she looked at Ian.

I'm telling you, if that was just friendship, my name's Gypsy Tirrasana!

And that's more or less the end of the story, except that a few days later a very confused Jan asked us all if we had any idea who Tanya Roberts was.

"Oh, it's me," I said, turning pink.

"In that case, you've got a letter," Jan said,

looking at me as though I'd lost my marbles as she handed me a small brown envelope.

"Let's see! Let's see!" said Luce, jumping up from the table and squashing herself in between Fen and me so she had the best possible view.

Andy was on duty, but she stopped work and leaned over on the other side between Leah and me. Jaimini stood behind her, and in this tight little semicircle we all read out loud the letter from the small brown envelope.

Dear Tanya,

My name is Doreen Carr and I was the fortune-teller at the fair at Cableden on Monday night. I presume you are the girl who came to see me in hospital. I am so glad you've written because I'd love to see you again now that I'm better.

When I was in hospital I think I told you that I sometimes get things right and I sometimes get things wrong. One thing I've obviously got wrong is your name. I thought it would be something beginning with T, but I guessed Tash, not Tanya, which just goes to prove my point.

My address and phone number are above and I would love to hear from you or your delightful mother, if you would like to get in touch.

Yours sincerely,
Doreen Carr.

"That's amazing," said Leah, and the others nodded silently. I think we were all a bit shell-shocked – well, all except Luce.

"Oh, great! Now we know where she lives," she said grinning round, "she can tell *all* our fortunes."

"No thanks," said four voices at once.

Join

Would you and your friends like to know more
about Fen, Tash, Leah, Andy, Jaimini and Luce?

We have produced a special bookmark for you to
use in your Café Club books. To get yours free,
together with a special newsletter about Fen and
her friends, their creator, author Ann Bryant,
and advance information about what's coming
next in the series, write (enclosing a self-
addressed label, please) to:

The Café Club
c/o the Publicity Department
Scholastic Children's Books
Commonwealth House
1-19 New Oxford Street
London WC1A 1NU

We look forward to hearing from you!

The CAFÉ Club

Make room for these delicious helpings
of the Café Club and meet the members:
Fen, Leah, Luce, Jaimini, Tash and
Andy. Work has never been so much fun!

1: GO FOR IT, FEN!
Fen and her friends are fed up with being poor.
Then Fen has a *brilliant* idea – she'll get them all
jobs in her aunt's café! *Nothing* can get in the way
of the Café Club...

2: LEAH DISCOVERS BOYS
What with the Café Club, homework and the Music
Festival, Leah certainly hasn't got time for *boyfriends*...
Until Oliver comes on the scene...

3: LUCE AND THE WEIRD KID
Nothing's working out for Luce. She's been grounded,
her hair's gone purple and now this weird kid's got
her into deep trouble at the café...

4: JAIMINI AND THE WEB OF LIES
Jaimini's parents want to ruin her life by sending
her to a posh school. But the Café Club are plotting
to save her...

5: ANDY THE PRISONER

Andy's a prisoner at creaky old Grandma Sorrell's!
She's got to break out – and she knows *just* the
friends to help her...

6: TASH'S SECRETS

Tash has a secret *no one* must find out about. If they
do, Tash might lose her friends for ever...

7: FEN'S REVENGE

Fen's having trouble with boys. She's out for revenge,
and the Café Club are right behind her...

8: LEAH IN TROUBLE

Leah needs cash, but Jan won't let her busk in the Café.
But then Jan falls ill, and Hilda Salmon takes over...

9: LUCE'S BIG MISTAKE

Luce can't believe she's too big to play Annie in
the musical! She's determined to get the part,
whatever the cost...

Don't forget to come back for more!

HIPPO ANIMAL

Have you ever longed for a puppy to love, or a horse of your own? Have you ever wondered what it would be like to make friends with a wild animal? If so, then you're sure to fall in love with these fantastic titles from Hippo Animal!

Thunderfoot
Deborah van der Beek
When Mel finds the enormous, neglected horse Thunderfoot, she doesn't know it will change her life for ever…

Vanilla Fudge
Deborah van der Beek
When Lizzie and Hannah fall in love with the same dog, neither of them will give up without a fight…

A Foxcub Named Freedom
Brenda Jobling
An injured vixen nudges her young son away from her. She can sense danger and cares nothing for herself – only for her son's freedom…

Goose on the Run
Brenda Jobling

It's an unusual pet – an injured Canada goose.
But soon Josh can't imagine being without him.
And the goose won't let *anyone* take him away
from Josh. . .

Pirate the Seal
Brenda Jobling

Ryan's always been lonely – but then he meets
Pirate and at last he has a real friend...

Animal Rescue
Bette Paul

Can Tessa help save the badgers of Delves Wood
from destruction?

Take Six Puppies
Bette Paul

Anna knows she shouldn't get attached to the
six new puppies at the Millington Farm Dog
Sanctuary, but surely it can't hurt to get just a
little bit fond of them...

ⵁIPPO GHOST

Summer Visitors
Emma thinks she's in for a really boring summer,
until she meets the Carstairs family on the beach.
But there's something very *strange* about her
new friends. . .
Carol Barton

Ghostly Music
Beth loves her piano lessons. So why have they
started to make her *ill*. . . ?
Richard Brown

A Patchwork of Ghosts
Who is the evil-looking ghost tormenting Lizzie,
and why does he want to hurt her...?
Angela Bull

The Ghosts who Waited
Everything's changed since Rosy and her family
moved house. Why has everyone suddenly
turned against her. . .?
Dennis Hamley

The Railway Phantoms
Rachel has visions. She dreams of two children
in strange, disintegrating clothes. And it seems
as if they are trying to contact her...
Dennis Hamley